Into the Unknown

Into the Unknown

Eleven Tales of Imagination

Edited by

Terry Carr

THOMAS NELSON INC.
Nashville / Camden / New York

Copyright © 1973 by Terry Carr

First edition

Library of Congress Cataloging in Publication Data

Carr, Terry, comp.
   Into the unknown.

    CONTENTS: Bradbury, R. McGillahee's brat.—Silverberg, R. As is.—Wyndham, J. Technical slip.—[etc.]
    1.   Short stories. [1. Fantasy. 2. Short stories] I. Title.
PZ5.C184In   [Fic]   73–7826
ISBN 0–8407–6342–5

Acknowledgments

McGILLAHEE'S BRAT by Ray Bradbury. Copyright © 1970 by Ray Bradbury. From *Fantasy & Science Fiction*, by permission of The Harold Matson Co., Inc.

AS IS by Robert Silverberg. Copyright © 1968 by Galaxy Publishing Corp. From *Worlds of Fantasy*, by permission of the author and his agents, Scott Mere-

Contents

Introduction

"Fantasy" is a word that has acquired misleading connotations; our rational, scientific upbringing suggests to us that fantasy stories are about unreal things. But while it's true that fantasy deals with the strange and the impossible, these are subjects that have a great deal to do with reality.

For one thing, fantasies help to define what is real, because they deal with things beyond the limits of everyday reality and in that way they make us aware of where the boundaries are. (Why do ghosts frighten us? Because they are inhabitants of Death, a realm that is still, as it was in Shakespeare's time, undiscovered by even the most knowledgeable among us.) And catching a glimpse of the normal world from outside can tell us things about its size and shape that we might never otherwise discover. (How do you suppose our world looks to a dog? Or to a god?)

But quite aside from that, there's the matter of what we are to consider "real." Of course vampires don't exist; neither do unicorns or leprechauns. But how unreal can something be if the very *idea* of it can frighten us, or give us hope, or make us laugh? Do we measure the reality of things by whether we can touch them with our fingertips or with our souls?

I think we do both, if we're wise. There are things and there are things, as my grandmother used to say.

9

To say that one kind of experience is real because we can do it again under predictable conditions is very scientific, and maybe that's how reality has to be defined on one level. But a great number of "unreal" things affect us strongly throughout our lives, so they must have their own kinds of reality.

This is a book of fantasy-realities. Some may make you feel uneasy; some may puzzle you; others may set you to laughing. And all of them, I hope, will bring you enjoyment.

—TERRY CARR

Oakland, California
November 2, 1972

McGillahee's Brat

BY RAY BRADBURY

*Ray Bradbury has to be at the head of any list
of the important modern fantasy writers. From
his short stories for* Weird Tales, *published in
the 1940's, through his famous books such as*
Fahrenheit 451 *and* The Illustrated Man, *Bradbury has told fascinating and distinguished
tales of the fantastic. Here is one of his latest—
and also one of his best: the story of a strange
child who refused to grow older.*

Jn 1953 I had spent six months in Dublin,
writing a screenplay. I had not been back since.

Now, fifteen years later, I had returned by boat,
train, and taxi, and here we pulled up in front of the
Royal Hibernian Hotel and here we got out and were
going up the front hotel steps when a beggar woman
shoved her filthy baby in our faces and cried:

"Ah, God, pity! It's pity we're in need of! Have you
some? !"

I had some somewhere on my person, and slapped
my pockets and fetched it out, and was on the point
of handing it over when I gave a small cry, or ex-
clamation. The coins spilled from my hand.

In that instant, the babe was eyeing me, and I the
babe.

Then it was snatched away. The woman bent to paw after the coins, glancing up at me in panic.

"What on earth?" My wife guided me up into the lobby where, stunned, standing at the register, I forgot my name. "What's wrong? What *happened* out there?"

"Did you see the baby?" I asked.

"The beggar's child—?"

"It's the same."

"The same *what*?"

"The same baby," I said, my lips numb, "that the woman used to shove in our faces fifteen years ago."

"Oh, come, now."

"Yes, come." And I went back to the door and opened it to look out.

But the street was empty. The beggar woman and her bundle had run off to some other street, some other hotel, some other arrival or departure.

I shut the door and went back to the register.

"What?" I said.

And suddenly remembering my name, wrote it down.

The child would not go away.

The memory, that is.

The recollection of other years and days in rains and fogs, the mother and her small creature, and the soot on that tiny face, and the cry of the woman herself which was like a shrieking of brakes put on to fend off damnation.

Sometimes, late at night, I heard her wailing as she went off the cliff of Ireland's weather and down upon rocks where the sea never stopped coming or going, but stayed forever in tumult.

But the child stayed, too.

My wife would catch me brooding at tea or after supper over the Irish coffee and say, *"That* again?"

"That."

"It's silly."

"Oh, it's silly, all right."

"You've always made fun of metaphysics, astrology, palmistry—"

"This is genetics."

"You'll spoil your whole vacation." My wife passed the apricot tarts and refilled my cup. "For the first time in years, we're traveling without a load of screenplays or novels. But out in Galway this morning you kept looking over your shoulder as if *she* were trotting in the road behind with her spitting image."

"Did I do that?"

"You know you did. You say genetics? That's good enough for me. That *is* the same woman begged out front of the hotel fifteen years ago, yes, but she has twenty children at home, each one inch shorter than the next, and all as alike as a bag of potatoes. Some families run like that. A gang of father's kids, or a gang of mother's absolute twins, and nothing in between. Yes, that child looks like the one we saw years back. But you look like your brother, don't you, and there's twelve years difference?"

"Keep talking," I said. "I feel better."

But that was a lie.

I went out to search the Dublin streets.

Oh, I didn't tell myself this, no. But, search I did.

From Trinity College on up O'Connell Street and

way around back to St. Stephen's Green I pretended a vast interest in fine architecture, but secretly watched for her and her dire burden.

I bumped into the usual haggle of banjo-pluckers and shuffle-dancers and hymn-singers and tenors gargling in their sinuses and baritones remembering a buried love or fitting a stone on their mother's grave, but nowhere did I surprise my quarry.

At last I approached the doorman at the Royal Hibernian Hotel.

"Mike," I said.

"Sir," said he.

"That woman who used to lurk about at the foot of the steps there—"

"Ah, the one with the babe, do you mean?"

"Do you know her! ?"

"Know her! Sweet Jesus, she's been the plague of my years since I was thirty, and look at the gray in my hair now!"

"She been begging *that* long?"

"And forever beyond."

"Her name—"

"Molly's as good as any. McGillahee, I think. Sure. McGillahee's it. Beg pardon, sir, why do you ask?"

"Have you *looked* at her baby, Mike?"

His nose winced at a sour smell. "Years back, I gave it up. These beggar women keep their kids in a dread style, sir, a condition roughly equivalent to the bubonic. They neither wipe nor bathe nor mend. Neatness would work against beggary, do you see? The fouler the better, that's the motto, eh?"

"Right. Mike, so you've never *really* examined the infant?"

"Aesthetics being a secret part of my life, I'm a

grcat one for averting the gaze. It's blind I am to help you, sir. Forgive."

"Forgiven, Mike." I passed him two shillings. "Oh . . . have you seen those two, lately?"

"Strange. Come to think, sir. They have not come here in . . ."—he counted on his fingers and showed surprise—"why, it must be ten days! They never done *that* before. Ten!"

"Ten," I said, and did some secret counting of my own. "Why, that would make it ever since the first day *I* arrived at the hotel."

"Do you *say* that now?"

"I say it, Mike."

And I wandered down the steps, wondering what I said and what I meant.

It was obvious she was hiding out.

I did not for a moment believe she or the child was sick.

Our collision in front of the hotel, the baby's eyes and mine striking flint, had startled her like a fox and shunted her off God-knows-where, to some other alley, some other town.

I smelled her evasion. She was a vixen, yes, but I felt myself, day by day, a better hound.

I took to walking earlier, later, in the strangest locales. I would leap off busses in Ballsbridge and prowl the fog or taxi half out to Kilcock and hide in pubs. I even knelt in Dean Swift's church to hear the echoes of his Houyhnhnm voice, but stiffened alert at the merest whimper of a child carried through.

It was all madness, to pursue such a brute idea. Yet on I went, itching where the damned thing scratched.

And then by sheer and wondrous accident in a

dousing downpour that smoked the gutters and fringed my hat with a million raindrops per second, while taking my nightly swim, it happened. . . .

Coming out of a Wally Beery 1930 vintage movie, some Cadbury's chocolate still in my mouth, I turned a corner. . . .

And this woman shoved a bundle in my face and cried a familiar cry:

"If there's mercy in your soul—!"

She stopped, riven. She spun about. She ran.

For in the instant, she *knew*. And the babe in her arms, with the shocked small face, and the swift bright eyes, he knew me, *too!* Both let out some kind of fearful cry.

God, how that woman could race.

I mean she put a block between her backside and me while I gathered breath to yell: "Stop, thief!"

It seemed an appropriate yell. The baby was a mystery I wished to solve. And there she vaulted off with it. I mean, she *seemed* a thief.

So I dashed after, crying, "Stop! Help! *You*, there!"

She kept a hundred yards between for the first half-mile, up over bridges across the Liffey and finally up Grafton Street, where I jogged into St. Stephen's Green to find it . . . empty.

She had absolutely vanished.

Unless, of course, I thought, turning in all directions, letting my gaze idle, it's into the Four Provinces pub she's gone . . .

There is where I went.

It was a good guess.

I shut the door quietly.

There, at the bar, was the beggar woman, putting a pint of Guinness to her own face, and giving a shot of gin to the babe for happy sucking.

I let my heart pound down to a slower pace, then took my place at the bar and said, "John Jamieson, please."

At my voice, the baby gave one kick. The gin sprayed from his mouth. He fell into a spasm of choked coughing.

The woman turned him over and thumped his back to stop the convulsion. The red face of the child faced me, eyes squeezed shut, mouth wide, and at last the seizure stopped, the cheeks grew less red, and I said:

"You there, baby."

There was a hush. Everyone in the bar waited.

I finished:

"You need a shave."

The babe flailed about in his mother's arms with a loud strange wounded cry, which I cut off with a simple:

"It's all right. I'm not the police."

The woman relaxed as if all her bones had gone to porridge.

"Put me down," said the babe.

She put him down on the floor.

"Give me my gin."

She handed him his little glass of gin.

"Let's go in the saloon bar where we can talk."

The babe led the way with some sort of small dignity, holding his swaddling clothes with one hand, and the gin glass in the other.

The saloon bar was empty, as he had guessed. The babe, without my help, climbed up into a chair at a table and finished his gin.

"Ah, Christ, I need another," he said in a tiny voice.

While his mother went to fetch a refill, I sat down and the babe and I eyed each other for a long moment.

"Well," he said at last, "what do ya think?"

"I don't know. I'm waiting and watching my own reactions," I said. "I may explode into laughter or tears at any moment."

"Let it be laughter. I couldn't stand the other."

On impulse, he stuck out his hand. I took it.

"The name is McGillahee. Better known as McGillahee's brat. Brat, for short."

"Brat," I said. "Smith."

He gripped my hand hard with his tiny fingers.

"Smith? Your name fits nothing. But Brat, well, don't a name like that go ten thousand leagues under? And what, you may ask, am I doing down here? And you up there so tall and fine and breathing the high air? Ah, but here's your drink, the same as mine. Put it in you, and listen."

The woman was back with shots for both. I drank, watched her, and said, "Are you the mother—?"

"It's me sister she is," said the babe. "Our mother's long since gone to her reward; a ha'penny a day for the next thousand years, nuppence dole from there on, and cold summers for a million years."

"Your sister? !" I must have sounded my disbelief, for she turned away to nibble her ale.

"You'd never guess, would you? She looks ten times my age. But if winter don't age you, Poor will. And winter and Poor is the whole tale. Porcelain cracks in this weather. And once she was the loveliest porcelain out of the summer oven." He gave her a gentle nudge. "But Mother she is now, for thirty years—"

"Thirty years you've been—!"

"Out front of the Royal Hibernian Hotel? And more! And our mother before that, and our father, too, and *his* father, the whole tribe! The day I was born, no sooner sacked in diapers, than I was on the street and my mother crying Pity and the world deaf, stone-dumb-blind and deaf. Thirty years with my sister, ten years with my mother, McGillahee's brat has been on display!"

"Forty?" I cried, and drank my gin to straighten my logic. "You're really forty? And all those years—how?"

"How did I get into this line of work?" said the babe. "You do not get, you are, as we say, *born* in. It's been nine hours a night, no Sundays off, no time clocks, no paychecks, and mostly dust and lint fresh paid out of the pockets of the rich."

"But I still don't understand," I said, gesturing to his size, his shape, his complexion.

"Nor will I, ever," said McGillahee's brat. "Am I a midget born to the blight? Some kind of dwarf shaped by glands? Or did someone warn me to play it safe, stay small?"

"That could hardly—"

"Couldn't it! It could! Listen. A thousand times I heard it, and a thousand times more my father came home from his beggary route and I remember him jabbing his finger in my crib, pointing at me, and saying, 'Brat, whatever you do, don't grow, not a muscle, not a hair! The Real Thing's out there; the World. You *hear* me, Brat? Dublin's beyond, and Ireland on top of that and England hard-assed above us all. It's not worth the consideration, the bother, the planning, the growing up to try and make do, so listen here, Brat; we'll stunt your growth with stories, with truth, with warnings and predictions, we'll wean you on gin, and smoke you with Spanish cigarettes until you're a cured Irish ham—pink, sweet, and small; small, do you hear, Brat? I did not want you in this world. But now you're in it, lie low, don't walk, creep; don't talk, wail; don't work, loll; and when the world is too much for you, Brat, give it back your opinion: *wet* yourself! Here, Brat, here's your evening poteen; fire it down. The Four Horsemen of the Apocalypse wait down by the Liffey. Would you see their like? Hang on. Here we go!'

"And out we'd duck for the evening rounds, my dad banging a banjo with me at his feet holding the cup, or him doing a tap dance, me under one arm, the musical instrument under the other, both making discord.

"Then, home late, we'd lie four in a bed, a crop of failed potatoes, discards of an ancient famine.

"And sometimes in the midst of the night, for lack of something to do, my father would jump out of bed in the cold and run out doors and fist his knuckles at the sky, I remember, I remember, I heard, I saw, daring God to lay hands on him, for so help him, Jesus, if *he* could lay hands on God, there would be torn feathers, ripped beards, lights put out, and the grand theatre of Creation shut tight for Eternity! do ya hear, God, ya dumb brute with your perpetual rainclouds turning their black behinds on me, do ya *care!* ?

"For answer, the sky wept, and my mother did the same all night, all night.

"And the next morn out I'd go again, this time in *her* arms and back and forth between the two, day on day, and her grieving for the million dead from the famine of 'fifty-one and him saying good-bye to the four million who sailed off to Boston. . . .

"Then one night, Dad vanished, too. Perhaps he sailed off on some mad boat like the rest, to forget us all. I forgive him. The poor beast was wild with hunger and nutty for want of something to give us and no giving.

"So then my mother simply washed away in her own tears, dissolved, you might say, like a sugar-crystal saint and was gone before the morning fog rolled back, and the grass took her, and my sister, aged twelve, overnight grew tall, but I, me, oh, me? I grew small. Each decided, you see, long before that, of course, on going his or her way.

"But then part of my decision happened early on. I knew, I swear I did! the quality of my own Thespian performance!

"I heard it from every decent beggar in Dublin when I was nine days old. 'What a beggar's babe *that* is!' they cried.

"And my mother, standing outside the Abbey Theatre in the rain when I was twenty and thirty days old, and the actors and directors coming out tuning their ears to my Gaelic laments, *they* said I should be signed up and trained! So the stage would have been mine with size, but size never came. And there's no brat's roles in Shakespeare. Puck, maybe; what else? So meanwhile at forty days and fifty nights after being born my performance made hackles rise and beggars yammer to borrow my hide, flesh, soul, and voice for an hour here, an hour there. The old lady rented me out by the half-day when she was sick abed. And not a one bought and bundled me off did not return with praise. My God, they cried, his yell would suck money from the Pope's poorbox!

"And outside the Cathedral one Sunday morn, an

American Cardinal was riven to the spot by the howl I gave when I saw his fancy skirt and bright cloth. Said he: 'That cry is the first cry of Christ at his birth, mixed with the dire yell of Lucifer churned out of Heaven and spilled in fiery muck down the landslide slops of Hell!'

"That's what the dear Cardinal said. Me, eh? Christ and the Devil in one lump, the gabble screaming out my mouth half lost, half found, can you *top* that?"

"I cannot," I said.

"Then, later on, many years further, there was this wild American film director who chased White Whales. The first time he spied me, he took a quick look and . . . winked! And took out a pound note and did not put it in my sister's hand, no, but took my own scabby fist and tucked the pound in and gave it a squeeze and another wink, and him gone.

"I seen his picture later in the paper, him stabbing the White Whale with a dread harpoon, and him proper mad, and I always figured, whenever we passed, he had my number, but I never winked back. I played the part dumb. And there was always a good pound in it for me, and him proud of my not giving in and letting him know that I knew that he knew.

"Of all the thousands who've gone by in the grand Ta-Ta! he was the only one ever looked me right in the eye, save you! The rest were all too embarrassed by life to so much as gaze as they put out the dole.

"Well, I mean now, what with that film director, and the Abbey players, and the cardinals and beggars telling me to go with my own natural self and talent and the genius busy in my babyfat, all *that* must have turned my head.

"Added to which, my having the famines tolled in

my ears, and not a day passed we did not see a funeral go by, or watch the unemployed march up and down in strikes, well, don't you see? Battered by rains and storms of people and knowing so much, I *must* have been driven down, driven back, don't you think?

"You cannot starve a babe and have a man; or do miracles run different than of old?

"My mind, with all the drear stuff dripped in my ears, was it likely to want to run around free in all that guile and sin and being put upon by natural nature and unnatural man? No. No! I just wanted my little cubby, and since I was long out of that, and no squeezing back, I just squinched myself small against the rains. I flaunted the torments.

"And, do you know? I won."

You did, Brat, I thought. You did.

"Well, I guess that's my story," said the small creature there perched on a chair in the empty saloon bar.

He looked at me for the first time since he had begun his tale.

The woman who was his sister, but seemed his gray mother, now dared to lift her gaze, also.

"Do," I said, "do the people of Dublin know about you?"

"Some. And envy me. And hate me, I guess, for getting off easy from God, and his plagues and Fates."

"Do the police know?"

"Who would tell them?"

There was a long pause.

Rain beat on the windows.

Somewhere a door hinge shrieked like a soul in torment as someone went out and someone else came in.

Silence.

"Not me," I said.

"Ah, Christ, Christ . . ."

And tears rolled down the sister's cheeks.

And tears rolled down the sooty strange face of the babe.

Both of them let the tears go, did not try to wipe them off, and at last they stopped, and we drank up the rest of our gin and sat a moment longer and then I said:

"The best hotel in town is the Royal Hibernian, the best for beggars, that is."

"True," they said.

"And for fear of meeting me, you've kept away from the richest territory?"

"We have."

"The night's young," I said. "There's a flight of rich ones coming in from Shannon just before midnight."

I stood up.

"If you'll let . . . I'll be happy to walk you there, now."

"The Saints' calendar is full," said the woman, "but somehow we'll find room for you."

Then I walked the woman McGillahee and her brat back through the rain toward the Royal Hibernian Hotel, and us talking along the way of the mobs of people coming in from the airport just before twelve, drinking and registering at that late hour, that fine hour for begging, and with the cold rain and all, not to be missed.

I carried the babe for some part of the way, she looking tired, and when we got in sight of the hotel, I handed him back, saying: "Is this the first time, ever?"

"We was found out by a Tourist? Aye," said the babe. "You have an otter's eye."

"I'm a writer."

"Nail me to the cross," said he, "I might have known! You won't—"

"No," I said. "I won't write a single word about this, about you, for another fifteen years or more."

"Mum's the word?"

"Mum."

We were a hundred feet from the hotel steps.

"I must shut up here," said Brat, lying there in his old sister's arms, fresh as peppermint candy from the gin, round-eyed, wild-haired, swathed in dirty linens and wools, small fists gently gesticulant. "We've a rule, Molly and me, no chat while at work. Grab my hand."

I grabbed the little fingers. It was like holding a sea anemone.

"God bless you," he said.

"And God," I said, "take care of you."

"Ah," said the babe, "in another year we'll have enough saved for the New York boat."

"We will," she said.

"And no more begging, and no more being the dirty babe crying by night in the storms, but some decent work in the open, do you know, do you see? Will you light a candle to that?"

"It's lit." I squeezed his hand.

"Go on ahead."

"I'm gone," I said.

And walked quickly to the front of the hotel, where airport taxis were starting to arrive.

Behind, I saw the woman trot forward, I saw her arms lift, with the Holy Child held out in the rain.

"If there's mercy in you!" she cried. "Pity—!"

And heard the coins ring in the cup and heard the sour babe wailing, and more cars coming and the woman crying Mercy and Thanks and Pity and God Bless and Praise Him and wiping tears from my own eyes, feeling eighteen inches tall, somehow made it up the high steps and into the hotel and to bed where rains fell cold on the rattled windows all the night and where, in the dawn, when I woke and looked out, the street was empty save for the steady falling storm.

As Is

BY ROBERT SILVERBERG

What used to be called used cars are now referred to as "fine previously owned automobiles," but you still have to be careful when you buy one. Robert Silverberg tells a curious and amusing tale of a man who got more of a bargain than he'd bargained for.

"*As is*," the auto dealer said, jamming his thumbs under his belt. "Two hundred fifty bucks and drive it away. I'm not pretending it's perfect, but I got to tell you, you're getting a damned good hunk of car for the price."

"As is," Sam Norton said.

"As is. Strictly as is."

Norton looked a little doubtful. "Maybe she drives well, but with a trunk that doesn't open—"

"So what?" the dealer snorted. "You told me yourself you're renting a U-Haul to get your stuff to California. What do you need a trunk for? Look, when you get out to the Coast and have a little time, take the car to a garage, tell 'em the story, and maybe five minutes with a blowtorch—"

"Why didn't you do that while you had the car in stock?"

The dealer looked evasive. "We don't have time to fool with details like that."

Norton let the point pass. He walked around the car again, giving it a close look from all angles. It was a smallish dark-green four-door sedan, with the finish and trim in good condition, a decent set of tires, and a general glow that comes only when a car has been well cared for. The upholstery was respectable, the radio was in working order, the engine was—as far as he could judge—okay, and a test drive had been smooth and easy. The car seemed to be a reasonably late model, too; it had shoulder-harness safety belts and emergency blinkers.

There was only one small thing wrong with it. The trunk didn't open. It wasn't just a case of a jammed lock, either; somebody had fixed this car so the trunk *couldn't* open. With great care the previous owner had apparently welded the trunk shut; nothing was visible back there except a dim line to mark the place where the lid might once have lifted.

What the hell, though. The car was otherwise in fine shape, and he wasn't in a position to be too picky. Overnight, practically, they had transferred him to the Los Angeles office, which was fine in terms of getting out of New York in the middle of a lousy winter, but not so good as far as his immediate finances went. The company didn't pay moving costs, only transportation; he had been handed four one-way tourist-class tickets, and that was that. So he had put Ellen and the kids aboard the first jet to L.A., cashing in his own ticket so he could use the money for the moving job. He figured to do it the slow but cheap way: rent a U-Haul trailer, stuff the family belongings into it, and set out via turnpike for California, hoping that Ellen had found an apartment by the time he got there. Only he couldn't trust his present clunker of a car to get him very far west of Parsippany, New Jersey, let alone through the Mojave Desert. So here he was, trying to pick up an honest used job for about five hundred bucks, which was all he could afford to lay out on the spot.

And here was the man at the used-car place offering him this very attractive vehicle—with its single peculiar defect—for only two and a half bills, which would leave him with that much extra cash cushion for the expenses of his transcontinental journey. And he didn't *really* need a trunk, driving alone. He could keep his suitcase on the back seat and stash everything else in the U-Haul. And it shouldn't be all that hard to have some mechanic in L.A. cut the trunk open for him and get it working again. On the other hand, Ellen was likely to chew him out for having bought a car that was sealed up that way; she had let him have it before on other "bargains" of that sort. On the third hand, the mystery of the sealed trunk appealed to him. Who knew what he'd find in there once he opened it up? Maybe the car had belonged to a smuggler who had had to hide a hot cargo fast, and the trunk was full of lovely golden ingots, or diamonds, or ninety-year-old cognac, which the smuggler had planned to reclaim a few weeks later, except that something unexpected had come up. On the fourth hand—

The dealer said, "How'd you like to take her out for another test spin, then?"

Norton shook his head. "Don't think I need to. I've got a good idea of how she rides."

"Well, then, let's step into the office and close the deal."

Sidestepping the maneuver, Norton said, "What year did you say she was?"

"Oh, about a 'sixty-four, 'sixty-five."

"You aren't sure?"

"You can't really tell with these foreign jobs, sometimes. You know, they don't change the model for five, six, ten years in a row, except in little ways that only an expert would notice. Take Volkswagen, for instance—"

"And I just realized," Norton cut in, "that you never told me what make she is, either."

"Peugeot, maybe, or some kind of Fiat," said the dealer hazily. "One of those kind."

"You don't *know*?"

A shrug. "Well, we checked a lot of the style books going back a few years, but there are so damn many of these foreign cars around, and some of them they import only a few thousand, and—well, so we couldn't quite figure it out."

Norton wondered how he was going to get spare parts for a car of unknown make and uncertain date. Then he realized that he was thinking of the car as his, already, even though the more he considered the deal, the less he liked it. And then he thought of those ingots in the trunk. The rare cognac. The suitcase full of rubies and sapphires.

He said, "Shouldn't the registration say something about the year and make?"

The dealer shifted his weight from foot to foot. "Matter of fact, we don't have the registration. But it's perfectly legitimate. Hey, look, I'd like to get this car out of my lot, so maybe we call it two twenty-five, huh?"

"It all sounds pretty mysterious. Where'd you get the car, anyway?"

"There was this little guy who brought it in, about a year ago, a year last November, I think it was. Give it a valve job, he said. I'll be back in a month—got to take a sudden business trip. Paid in advance for tune-up and a month's storage and everything. Wouldn't you know that was the last we ever saw of him? Well, we stored his damn car here free for ten, eleven months, but that's it, now we got to get it out of the place. The lawyer says we can take possession for the storage charge."

"If I buy it, you give me a paper saying you had the right to sell it?"

"Sure. Sure."

"And what about getting the registration? Shifting the insurance over from my old heap? All the red tape?"

"I'll handle everything," the dealer said. "Just you take the car outa here."

"Two hundred," Norton said. "As is."

The dealer sighed. "It's a deal. As is."

A light snow was falling when Norton began his cross-country hegira three days later. It was an omen, but he was not sure what kind; he decided that the snow was intended as his last view of a dreary winter phenomenon he wouldn't be seeing again, for a while. According to the *Times*, yesterday's temperature range in L.A. had been sixty-six low, seventy-nine high. Not bad for January.

He slouched down behind the wheel, let his foot rest lightly on the accelerator, and sped westward at a sane, sensible forty-five miles per hour. That was about as fast as he dared go with the bulky

U-Haul trailing behind. He hadn't had much experience driving with a trailer—he was a computer salesman, and computer salesmen don't carry sample computers—but he got the hang of it pretty fast. You just had to remember that your vehicle was now a segmented organism, and make your turns accordingly. God bless turnpikes, anyhow. Just drive on, straight and straight and straight, heading toward the land of the sunset with only a few gentle curves and half a dozen traffic lights along the way.

The snow thickened some. But the car responded beautifully, hugging the road, and the windshield wipers kept his view clear. He hadn't expected to buy a foreign car for the trip at all; when he had set out, it was to get a good solid Plymouth or Chevvie, something heavy and sturdy to take him through the wide open spaces. But he had no regrets about this smaller car. It had all the power and pickup he needed, and with that trailer bouncing along behind him he wouldn't have much use for all that extra horsepower, anyway.

He was in a cheerful, relaxed mood. The car seemed comforting and protective, a warm enclosing environment that would contain and shelter him through the thousands of miles ahead. He was still close enough to New York to be able to get Mozart on the radio, which was nice. The car's heater worked well. There wasn't much traffic. The snow itself, new and white and fluffy, was all the more beautiful for the knowledge that he was leaving it behind. He even enjoyed the solitude. It would be restful, in a way, driving on and on through Ohio and Kansas and Colorado or Arizona or whatever states lay between him and Los Angeles. Five or six days of peace and quiet, no need to make small talk, no kids to amuse—

His frame of mind began to darken not long after he got on the Pennsylvania Turnpike. If you have enough time to think, you will eventually think of the things you should have thought of before; and now, as he rolled through the thickening snow on this gray and silent afternoon, certain aspects of a trunkless car occurred to him that in his rush to get on the road he had succeeded in overlooking earlier. What about a tool kit, for instance? If he had a flat, what would he use for a jack and a wrench? That led him to a much more chilling thought: what would he use for a spare tire? A trunk was something more than a cavity back of the rear seat; in most cars it contained highly useful objects.

None of which he had with him.

None of which he had even thought about, until just this minute.

He contemplated the prospects of driving from coast to coast without a spare tire and without tools, and his mood of warm security evaporated abruptly. At the next exit, he decided, he'd hunt for a service station and pick up a tire, fast. There would be room for it on the back seat next to his luggage. And while he was at it, he might as well buy—

The U-Haul, he suddenly observed, was jackknifing around awkwardly in back, as though its wheels had just lost traction. A moment later the car was doing the same, and he found himself moving laterally in a beautiful skid across an unsanded slick patch on the highway. Steer in the direction of the skid, that's what you're supposed to do, he told himself, strangely calm. Somehow he managed to keep his foot off the brake despite all natural inclinations, and watched in quiet horror as car and trailer slid placidly across the empty lane to his right and came to rest, upright and facing forward, in the piled-up snowbank along the shoulder of the road.

He let out his breath slowly, scratched his chin, and gently fed some gas. The spinning wheels made a high-pitched whining sound against the snow. He went nowhere. He was stuck.

The little man had a ruddy-cheeked face, white hair so long it curled at the ends, and metal-rimmed spectacles. He glanced at the snow covered autos in the used-car lot, scowled, and trudged toward the showroom.

"Came to pick up my car," he announced. "Valve job. Delayed by business in another part of the world."

The dealer looked uncomfortable. "The car's not here."

"So I see. Get it, then."

"We more or less sold it about a week ago."

"*Sold it?* Sold my car? *My car?*"

"Which you abandoned. Which we stored here for a whole year. This ain't no parking lot here. Look, I talked to my lawyer first, and he said—"

"All right. All right. Who was the purchaser?"

"A guy, he was transferred to California and had to get a car fast to drive out. He—"

"His name?"

"Look, I can't tell you that. He bought the car in good faith. You got no call bothering him now."

The little man said, "If I chose, I could draw the information from you in a number of ways. But never mind. I'll locate the car easily enough. And you'll certainly regret this scandalous breach of custodial duties. You certainly shall."

He went stamping out of the showroom, muttering indignantly.

Several minutes later a flash of lightning blazed across the sky. "Lightning?" the auto dealer wondered. "In January? During a snowstorm?"

When the thunder came rumbling in, every pane of plate glass in every window of the showroom shattered and fell out in the same instant.

U. S. **1772948**

Sam Norton sat spinning his wheels for a while in mounting fury. He knew it did no good, but he wasn't sure what else he could do, at this point, except hit the gas and hope for the car to pull itself out of the snow. His only other hope was for the highway patrol to come along, see his plight, and summon a tow truck. But the highway was all but empty, and those few cars that drove by shot past him without stopping.

When ten minutes had passed, he decided to have a closer look at the situation. He wondered vaguely if he could somehow scuff away enough snow with his foot to allow the wheels to get a little purchase. It didn't sound plausible, but there wasn't much else he could do. He got out and headed to the back of the car.

And noticed for the first time that the trunk was open.

The lid had popped up about a foot, along that neat welded line of demarcation. In astonishment Norton pushed it higher and peered inside.

The interior had a dank, musty smell. He couldn't

see much of what might be in there, for the light was dim and the lid would lift no higher. It seemed to him that there were odd lumpy objects scattered about, objects of no particular size or shape, but he felt nothing when he groped around. He had the impression that the things in the trunk were moving away from his hand, vanishing into the darkest corners as he reached for them. But then his fingers encountered something cold and smooth, and he heard a welcome clink of metal on metal. He pulled.

A set of tire chains came forth.

He grinned at his good luck. Just what he needed! Quickly he unwound the chains and crouched by the back wheels of the car to fasten them in place. The lid of the trunk slammed shut as he worked—hinge must be loose, he thought—but that was of no importance. In five minutes he had the chains attached. Getting behind the wheel, he started the car again, fed some gas, delicately let in the clutch, and bit down hard on his lower lip by way of helping the car out of the snowbank. The car eased forward until it was in the clear. He left the chains on until he reached a service area eight miles up the turnpike. There he undid them; and when he stood up, he found that the trunk had popped open again. Norton tossed the chains inside and knelt in another attempt to see what else might be in the trunk; but not even by squinting did he discover anything. When he touched the lid, it snapped shut, and once more the rear of the car presented that puzzling welded-tight look.

Mine not to reason why, he told himself. He headed into the station and asked the attendant to sell him a spare tire and a set of tools. The attendant, frowning a bit, studied the car through the station window and said, "Don't know as we got one to fit. We got standards and we got smalls, but you got an in-between. Never saw a size tire like that, really."

"Maybe you ought to take a closer look," Norton suggested. "Just in case it's really a standard foreign-car size, and—"

"Nope. I can see from here. What you driving, anyway? One of them Japanese jobs?"

"Something like that."

"Look, maybe you can get a tire in Harrisburg. They got a place there, it caters to foreign cars, get yourself a muffler, shocks, anything you need."

"Thanks," Norton said, and went out.

He didn't feel like stopping when the turnoff for Harrisburg came by. It made him a little queasy to be driving without a spare, but somehow he wasn't as worried about it as he'd been before. The trunk had had tire chains when he needed them. There was no telling what else might turn up back there at the right time. He drove on.

Since the little man's own vehicle wasn't available to him, he had to arrange a rental. That was no problem, though. There were agencies in every city that specialized in such things. Very shortly he was in touch with one, not exactly by telephone, and was explaining his dilemma. "The difficulty," the little man said, "is that he's got a head start of several days. I've traced him to a point west of Chicago, and he's moving forward at a pretty steady four hundred fifty miles a day."

"You'd better fly, then."

"That's what I've been thinking, too," said the little man. "What's available fast?"

"Could have given you a nice Persian job, but it's out having its tassels restrung. But you don't care much for carpets anyway, do you? I forgot."

"Don't trust 'em in thermals," said the little man. "I caught an updraft once in Sikkim and I was half-way up the Himalayas before I got things under control. Looked for a while like I'd end up in orbit. What's at the stable?"

"Well, some pretty decent jobs. There's this classy stallion that's been resting up all winter, though actually he's a little cranky—maybe you'd prefer the bay gelding. Why don't you stop around and decide for yourself?"

"Will do," the little man said. "You still take Diner's Club, don't you?"

"All major credit cards, as always. You bet."

Norton was in southern Illinois, an hour out of St. Louis on a foggy, humid morning, when the front right-hand tire blew. He had been expecting it to go for a day and a half, now, ever since he'd stopped in Altoona for gas. The kid at the service station had tapped the tire's treads and showed him the weak spot, and Norton had nodded and asked about his chances of buying a spare, and the kid had shrugged and said, "It's a funny size. Try in Pittsburgh, maybe." He tried in Pittsburgh, killing an hour and a half there, and hearing from several men who probably ought to know that tires just weren't made to that size, nohow. Norton was beginning to wonder how the previous owner of the car had managed to find replacements. Maybe this was still the original set, he figured. But he was morbidly sure of one thing: that weak spot was going to give out, beyond any doubt, before he saw L.A.

When it blew, he was doing about thirty-five, and he realized at once what had happened. He slowed the car to a halt without losing control. The shoulder was wide here, but even so Norton was grateful that the flat was on the right-hand side of the car; he didn't much feature having to change a tire with his rump to the traffic. He was still congratulating himself on that small bit of good luck when he remembered that he had no spare tire.

Somehow he couldn't get very disturbed about it. Spending a dozen hours a day behind the wheel was evidently having a tranquilizing effect on him; at this point nothing worried him much, not even the prospect of being stranded an hour east of St. Louis. He would merely walk to the nearest telephone, wherever that might happen to be, and he would phone the local automobile club and explain his predicament, and they would come out and get him and tow him to civilization. Then he would settle in a motel for a day or two, phoning Ellen at her sister's place in L.A. to say that he was all right but was going to be a little late. Either he would have the tire patched or the automobile club would find a place in St. Louis that sold odd sizes, and everything would turn out for the best. Why get into a dither?

He stepped out of the car and inspected the flat, which looked very flat indeed. Then, observing that the trunk had popped open again, he went around back. Reaching in experimentally, he expected to find the tire chains at the outer edge of the trunk, where he had left them. They weren't there. Instead his fingers closed on a massive metal bar. Norton tugged it partway out of the trunk and discovered that he had found a jack. Exactly so, he thought. And the spare tire ought to be right in back of it, over here, yes? He looked, but the lid was up only eighteen inches or so, and he couldn't see much. His fingers encountered good rubber, though. Yes, here it is. Nice and plump, brand new, deep treads—very pretty. And next to it, if my luck holds, I ought to find a chest of golden doubloons—

The doubloons weren't there. Maybe next time, he told himself. He hauled out the tire and spent a sweaty half hour putting it on. When he was done, he dumped the jack, the wrench, and the blown tire into the trunk, which immediately shut to the usual hermetic degree of sealing. An hour later, without further incident, he crossed the Mississippi into St. Louis, found a room in a shiny new motel overlooking the Gateway Arch, treated himself to a hot shower and a couple of cold Gibsons, and put in a collect call to Ellen's sister. Ellen had just come back from some unsuccessful apartment hunting, and she sounded tired and discouraged. Children were howling in the background as she said, "You're driving carefully, aren't you?"

"Of course I am."

"And the new car is behaving okay?"

"Its behavior," Norton said, "is beyond reproach."

"My sister wants to know what kind it is. She says a Volvo is a good kind of car, if you want a foreign car. That's a Norwegian car."

"Swedish," he corrected.

He heard Ellen say to her sister, "He bought a Swedish car." The reply was unintelligible, but a moment later Ellen said, "She says you did a smart thing. Those Swedes, they make good cars too."

The flight ceiling was low, with visibility less than half a mile in thick fog. Airports were socked in all over Pennsylvania and eastern Ohio. The little man flew westward, though, keeping just above the fleecy whiteness spreading to the horizon. He was making good time, and it was a relief not to have to worry about those damned private planes.

The bay gelding had plenty of stamina, too. He was a fuel-guzzler, that was his only trouble. You didn't get a whole lot of miles to the bale with the horses available nowadays, the little man thought sadly. Everything was in a state of decline, and you had to accept the situation.

His original flight plan had called for him to overtake his car somewhere in the Texas Panhandle. But he had stopped off in Chicago on a sudden whim to visit friends, and now he calculated he wouldn't catch up with the car until Arizona. He couldn't wait to get behind the wheel again, after all these months.

The more he thought about the trunk and the tricks it had played, the more bothered by it all Sam Norton was. The chains, the spare tire, the jack—what next? In Amarillo he had offered a mechanic twenty bucks to get the trunk open. The mechanic had run his fingers along that smooth seam in disbelief. "What are you, one of those television fellers?" he asked. "Having some fun with me?"

"Not at all," Norton said. "I just want that trunk opened up."

"Well, I reckon maybe with an acetylene torch—"

But Norton felt an obscure terror at the idea of cutting into the car that way. He didn't know why the thought frightened him so much, but it did, and he drove out of Amarillo with the car whole and the mechanic muttering and spraying his boots with tobacco juice. A hundred miles on, when he was over the New Mexico border and moving through bleak, forlorn, winter-browned country, he decided to put the trunk to a test.

LAST GAS BEFORE ROSWELL, a peeling sign warned. FILL UP NOW!

The gas gauge told him that the tank was nearly empty. Roswell was somewhere far ahead. There wasn't another human being in sight, no town, not even a shack. This, Norton decided, is the right place to run out of gas.

He shot past the gas station at fifty miles an hour.

In a few minutes he was two and a half mountains away from the filling station and beginning to have doubts not merely of the wisdom of his course but even of his sanity. Deliberately letting himself run out of gas was against all reason; it was harder even to do than deliberately letting the telephone go unanswered. A dozen times he ordered himself to swing around and go back to fill his tank, and a dozen times he refused.

The needle crept lower, until it was reading E for Empty, and still he drove ahead. The needle slipped through the red warning zone below the E. He had used up even the extra couple of gallons of gas that the tank didn't register—the safety margin for careless drivers. And any moment now the car would—

—stop.

For the first time in his life Sam Norton had run out of gas. Okay, trunk, let's see what you can do, he thought. He pushed the door open and felt the chilly zip of the mountain breeze. It was quiet here, ominously so; except for the gray ribbon of the road itself, this neighborhood had a darkly prehistoric look, all sagebrush and pinyon pine and not a trace of man's impact. Norton walked around to the rear of his car.

The trunk was open again.

It figures. Now I reach inside and find that a ten-gallon can of gas has mysteriously materialized, and—

He couldn't feel any can of gas in the trunk. He groped a good long while and came up with nothing more useful than a coil of thick rope.

Rope?

What good is rope to a man who's out of gas in the desert?

Norton hefted the rope, seeking answers from it and not getting any. It occurred to him that perhaps this time the trunk hadn't *wanted* to help him. The skid, the blowout—those hadn't been his fault. But he had with malice aforethought let the car run out of gas, just to see what would happen, and maybe that didn't fall within the scope of the trunk's services.

Why the rope, though?

Some kind of grisly joke? Was the trunk telling him to go string himself up? He couldn't even do that properly here; there wasn't a tree in sight tall enough for a man to hang himself from, not even a telephone pole. Norton felt like kicking himself. Here he was, and here he'd remain for hours, maybe even for days, until another car came along. Of all the dumb stunts!

Angrily he hurled the rope into the air. It uncoiled as he let go of it, and one end rose straight up. The rope hovered about a yard off the ground, rigid, pointing skyward. A faint turquoise cloud formed at the upper end, and a thin, muscular olive-skinned boy in a turban and a loincloth climbed down to confront the gaping Norton.

"Well, what's the trouble?" the boy asked brusquely.

"I'm . . . out . . . of . . . gas."

"There's a filling station twenty miles back. Why didn't you tank up there?"

"I . . . that is . . ."

"What a damned fool," the boy said in disgust. "Why do I get stuck with jobs like this? All right, don't go anywhere and I'll see what I can do."

He went up the rope again and vanished.

When he returned, some three minutes later, he was carrying a tin of gasoline. Glowering at Norton, he slid the gas-tank cover aside and poured in the gas.

"This'll get you to Roswell," he said. "From now on look at your dashboard once in a while. Idiot!"

He scrambled up the rope. When he disappeared, the rope went limp and fell. Norton shakily picked it up and slipped it into the trunk, whose lid shut with an aggressive slam.

Half an hour went by before Norton felt it was safe to get behind the wheel again. He paced around the car something more than a thousand times, not getting a whole lot steadier in the nerves, and ultimately, with night coming on, got in and switched on the ignition. The engine coughed and turned over. He began to drive toward Roswell at a sober and steadfast fifteen miles an hour.

He was willing to believe anything, now.

And so it did not upset him at all when a handsome reddish-brown horse with the wingspread of a DC-3 came soaring through the air, circled above the car a couple of times, and made a neat landing on the highway alongside him. The horse trotted along, keeping pace with him, while the small white-haired man in the saddle yelled, "Open your window wider, young fellow! I've got to talk to you!"

Norton opened the window.

The little man said, "Your name Sam Norton?"

"That's right."

"Well, listen, Sam Norton, you're driving my car!"

Norton saw a dirt turnoff up ahead and pulled into it. As he got out, the pegasus came trotting up and halted to let its rider dismount. It cropped moodily at sagebrush, fluttering its huge wings a couple of times before folding them neatly along its back.

The little man said, "My car, all right. Had her specially made a few years back, when I was on the road a lot. Dropped her off at the garage last winter account of I had a business trip to make abroad, but I never figured they'd sell her out from under me before I got back. It's a decadent age, that's the truth."

"Your . . . car . . ." Norton said.

"My car, yep. Afraid I'll have to take it from you, too. Car like this, you don't want to own it, anyway.

Too complicated. Get yourself a decent little standard-make flivver, eh? Well, now, let's unhitch this trailer thing of yours, and then—"

"Wait a second," Norton said. "I bought this car legally. I've got a bill of sale to prove it, and a letter from the dealer's lawyer, explaining that—"

"Don't matter one bit," said the little man. "One crook hires another crook to testify to his character, that's not too impressive. I know you're an innocent party, son, but the fact remains that the car is my property, and I hope I don't have to use special persuasion to get you to relinquish it."

"You just want me to get out and walk, is that it? In the middle of the New Mexico desert at sundown? Dragging the damned U-Haul with my bare hands?"

"Hadn't really considered that problem much," the little man said. "Wouldn't altogether be fair to you, would it?"

"It sure wouldn't." He thought a moment. "And what about the two hundred bucks I paid for the car?"

The little man laughed. "Shucks, it cost me more than that to rent the pegasus to come chasing you! And the overhead! You know how much hay that critter—"

"That's your problem," Norton said. "Mine is that you want to strand me in the desert and that you want to take away a car that I bought in good faith for two hundred dollars, and even if it's a goddam magic car I—"

"Hush, now," said the little man. "You're gettin' all upset, Sam! We can work this thing out. You're going to L.A., that it?"

"Ye-es."

"So am I. Okay, we travel together. I'll deliver you and your trailer, here, and then the car's mine again, and you forget anything you might have seen these last few days."

"And my two hundred dol—"

"Oh, all right." The little man walked to the back of the car. The trunk opened; he slipped in a hand and pulled forth a sheaf of crisp new bills, a dozen twenties, which he handed to Norton. "Here. With a little something extra, thrown in. And don't look at them so suspiciously, hear? That's good legal tender U.S. money. They even got different serial numbers, every one." He winked and strolled over to the grazing pegasus, which he slapped briskly on the rump. "Git along, now. Head for home. You cost me enough already!"

The horse began to canter along the highway. As it broke into a gallop it spread its superb wings; they beat furiously a moment, and the horse took off, rising in a superb arc until it was no bigger than a hawk against the darkening sky, and then was gone.

The little man slipped into the driver's seat of the car and fondled the wheel in obvious affection. At a nod, Norton took the seat beside him, and off they went.

"I understand you peddle computers," the little man said when he had driven a couple of miles. "Mighty interesting things, computers. I've been considering computerizing our operation too, you know? It's a pretty big outfit, a lot of consulting stuff all over the world, mostly dowsing now, some thaumaturgy, now and then a little transmutation, things like that, and though we use traditional methods we don't object to the scientific approach. Now, let me tell you a bit about our inventory flow, and maybe you can make a few intelligent suggestions, young fellow, and you might just be landing a nice contract for yourself—"

Norton had the roughs for the system worked out before they hit Arizona. From Phoenix he phoned Ellen and found out that she had rented an apartment just outside Beverly Hills, in what *looked* like a terribly expensive neighborhood but really wasn't, at least, not by comparison with some of the other things she'd seen, and—

"It's okay," he said. "I'm in the process of closing a pretty big sale. I . . . ah . . . picked up a hitchhiker, and turns out he's thinking of going computer soon, a fairly large company—"

"Sam, you haven't been drinking, have you?"

"Not a drop."

"A hitchhiker and you sold him a computer. Next you'll tell me about the flying saucer you saw."

"Don't be silly," Norton said. "Flying saucers aren't real."

They drove into L.A. in midmorning, two days later. By then he had written the whole order, and everything was set; the commission, he figured, would be enough to see him through a new car, maybe one of those Swedish jobs Ellen's sister had heard about. The little man seemed to have no difficulty finding the address of the apartment Ellen had taken; he negotiated the maze of the freeways with complete ease and assurance, and pulled up outside the house.

"Been a most pleasant trip, young fellow," the

little man said. "I'll be talking to my bankers later today about that wonderful machine of yours. Meanwhile here we part. You'll have to unhitch the trailer, now."

"What am I supposed to tell my wife about the car I drove here in?"

"Oh, just say that you sold it to that hitchhiker at a good profit. I think she'll appreciate that."

They got out. While Norton undid the U-Haul's couplings, the little man took something from the trunk, which had opened a moment before. It was a large rubbery tarpaulin. The little man began to spread it over the car. "Give us a hand here, will you?" he said. "Spread it nice and neat, so it covers the fenders and everything." He got inside, while Norton, baffled, carefully tucked the tarpaulin into place.

"You want me to cover the windshield too?" he asked.

"Everything," said the little man, and Norton covered the windshield. Now the car was wholly hidden.

There was a hissing sound, as of air being let out of tires. The tarpaulin began to flatten. As it sank toward the ground, there came a cheery voice from underneath, calling, "Good luck, young fellow!"

In moments the tarpaulin was less than three feet high. In a minute more it lay flat against the pavement. There was no sign of the car. It might have evaporated, or vanished into the earth. Slowly, uncomprehendingly, Norton picked up the tarpaulin, folded it until he could fit it under his arm, and walked into the house to tell his wife that he had arrived in Los Angeles.

Sam Norton never met the little man again, but he made the sale, and the commission saw him through a new car with something left over. He still has the tarpaulin, too. He keeps it folded up and carefully locked away in his basement. He's afraid to get rid of it, but he doesn't like to think of what might happen if someone came across it and spread it out.

Technical Slip

By John Wyndham

John Wyndham, who wrote The Day of the
Triffids, *offers an intriguing story of a man
given the chance to relive his life—but this
time he knew the future, since he could remember it. What might he do with such knowledge? Well, what would* you *do?*

"Prendergast," said the Departmental Director, briskly, "there'll be that Contract XB2832 business
arising today. Look after it, will you?"
"Very good, sir."

Robert Finnerson lay dying. Two or three times
before he had been under the impression that he
might be dying. He had been frightened, and blus-
terously opposed to the idea, but this time it was
different; he did not bluster, for he had no doubt
that the time had come. Even so, he was still opposed;
it was under marked protest that he acknowledged the
imminence of the nonsensical arrangement.

It was absurd to die at sixty, anyway, and, as he
saw it, it would be even more wasteful to die at
eighty. A scheme of things in which the wisdom
acquired in living was simply scrapped in this way

51

was, to say the least, grossly inefficient. What did it mean? That somebody else would now have to go through the process of learning all that life had already taken sixty years to teach him; and then be similarly scrapped in the end. No wonder the race was slow in getting anywhere—if, indeed, it was getting anywhere—with this cat-and-mouse, ten-forward-and-nine-back system.

Lying back on one's pillows and waiting for the end in the quiet, dim room, the whole ground plan of existence appeared to suffer from a basic futility of conception. It was a matter to which some of these illustrious scientists might well pay more attention—only, of course, they were always too busy fiddling with less important matters, until they came to his present pass, when they would find it was too late to do anything about it.

Since his reflections had revolved thus purposelessly, and several times, upon somewhat elliptical orbits, it was not possible for him to determine at which stage of them he became aware that he was no longer alone in the room. The feeling simply grew that there was someone else there, and he turned his head on the pillow to see who it might be. The thin, clerkly man whom he found himself regarding was unknown to him and yet, somehow, unsurprising.

"Who are you?" Robert Finnerson asked him.

The man did not reply immediately. He looked about Robert's own age, with a face kindly but undistinguished beneath hair that had thinned and grayed. His manner was diffident, but the eyes which regarded Robert through modest gold-rimmed spectacles were observant.

"Pray do not be alarmed, Mr. Finnerson," he requested.

"I'm not at all alarmed," Robert told him testily. "I simply asked who you are."

"My name is Prendergast—not, of course, that that matters—."

"Never heard of you. What do you want?" Robert said.

Prendergast told him modestly:

"My employers wish to lay a proposition before you, Mr. Finnerson."

"Too late now for propositions," Robert replied shortly.

"Ah, yes, for most propositions, of course, but I think this one may interest you."

"I don't see how—all right, what is it?"

"Well, Mr. Finnerson, we—that is, my employers —find that you are . . . er . . . scheduled for demise on April twentieth, nineteen sixty-three. That is, of course, tomorrow."

"Indeed," said Robert calmly, and with a feeling that he should have been more surprised than he felt. "I had come to much the same conclusion myself."

"*Quite*, sir," agreed the other. "But our information also is that you are opposed to this . . . er . . . schedule."

"Indeed!" repeated Mr. Finnerson. "How subtle! If that's all you have to tell me, Mr. Pendlebuss—."

"Prendergast, sir. No, that is just by way of assuring you of our grasp of the situation. We are also aware that you are a man of considerable means, and, well, there's an old saying that 'you can't take it with you,' Mr. Finnerson."

Robert Finnerson looked at his visitor more closely.

"Just what are you getting at?" he inquired.

"Simply this, Mr. Finnerson. My firm is in a position to offer a revision of schedule—for a consideration."

Robert was already far enough from his normal for the improbability. It did not occur to him to question its possibility. He said:

"What revision—and what consideration?"

"Well, there are several alternative forms," explained Prendergast, "but the one we recommend for your consideration is our Reversion Policy. It is quite our most comprehensive benefit—introduced originally on account of the large numbers of persons in positions similar to yours who were noticed to express the wish 'if only I had my life to live over again.'"

"I see," said Robert, and indeed he did. The fact that he had read somewhere or other of legendary bargains of the kind went a long way to disperse the unreality of the situation. "And the catch is?" he added.

Prendergast allowed a trace of disapproval to show.

"The *consideration*," he said with some slight stress upon the word. "The consideration in respect of a Reversion is a down payment to us of seventy-five per cent of your present capital."

"Seventy-five per cent! What is this firm of yours?"

Prendergast shook his head.

"You would not recall it, but it is a very old-established concern. We have had—and do have—numbers of notable clients. In the old days we used to work on a basis of—well—I suppose you would call it barter. But with the rise of commerce we changed our methods. We have found it much more

convenient to have investable capital than to ac-
cumulate souls—especially at their present de-
pressed market value. It is a great improvement in
all ways. We benefit considerably, and it costs you
nothing but money you must lose anyway—and you
are still entitled to call your soul your own; as far,
that is, as the law of the land permits. Your heirs
will be a trifle disappointed, that's all."

The last was not a consideration to distress Robert
Finnerson.

"My heirs are around the house like vultures already," he said. "I don't in the least mind their
having a little shock. Let's get down to details, Mr.
Snodgrass."

"Prendergast," said the visitor, patiently. "Well
now, the usual method of payment is this. . . ."

It was a whim, or what appeared to be a whim,
which impelled Mr. Finnerson to visit Sands Square.
Many years had passed since he had seen it, and
though the thought of a visit had risen from time to
time, there had seemed never to be the leisure. But
now in the convalescence which followed the remarkable, indeed miraculous recovery which had
given such disappointment to his relatives, he found
himself for the first time in years with an abundance
of spare hours on his hands.

He dismissed the taxi at the corner of the Square
and stood for some minutes surveying the scene with
mixed feelings. It was both smaller and shabbier
than his memory of it. Smaller, partly because most
things seem smaller when revisited after a stretch of
years, and partly because the whole of the south side
including the house which had been his home was

now occupied by an overbearing block of offices; shabbier because the new block emphasized the decrepitude of those Georgian terraces which had survived the bombs and had therefore had to outlast their expected span by twenty or thirty years.

But if most things had shrunk, the trees now freshly in leaf had grown considerably, seeming to crowd the sky with their branches, though there were fewer of them. A change was the bright banks of color from tulips in well-tended beds that had grown nothing but tired-looking laurels before. Greatest change of all, the garden was no longer forbidden to all but the residents, for the iron railings so long employed in protecting the privileged had gone for scrap in 1941 and never been replaced.

In a recollective mood and with a trace of melancholy, Mr. Finnerson crossed the road and began to stroll again along the once familiar paths. It pleased and yet saddened him to discover the semi-concealed gardener's shed looking just as it had looked fifty years ago. It displeased him to notice the absence of the circular seat that used to surround the trunk of a familiar tree. He wandered on, noting this and remembering that, but in general remembering too much, and beginning to regret that he had come. The garden was pleasant—better looked after than it had been—but, for him, too full of ghosts. Overall there was a sadness of glory lost, with a surrounding shabbiness.

On the east side a well-remembered knoll survived. It was, he recalled as he walked slowly up it, improbably reputed to be a last fragment of the earthworks which London had prepared against the threat of Royalist attack.

In the circle of bushes that crowned it, a hard, slatted chair rested in seclusion. The fancy took him to hide in this spot as he had been wont to hide there half a century before. With his handkerchief he dusted away the pigeon droppings and the looser grime. The relief he found in the relaxation of sitting down made him wonder if he had not been over-estimating his recuperation. He felt quite unusually weary. . . .

Peace was splintered by a girl's insistent voice.

"Bobby!" she called. "Master Bobby, where are you?"

Mr. Finnerson was irritated. The voice jarred on him. He tried to disregard it as it called again.

Presently a head appeared among the surrounding bushes. The face was a girl's; above it a bonnet of dark-blue straw; around it navy-blue ribbons, joining in a bow on the left cheek. It was a pretty face, though at the moment it wore a professional frown.

"Oh, there you are, you naughty boy. Why didn't you answer when I called?"

Mr. Finnerson looked behind him to find the child addressed. There was none. As he turned back he became aware that the chair had gone. He was sitting on the ground, and the bushes seemed taller than he had thought.

"Come along now. You'll be late for your tea," added the girl. She seemed to be looking at Mr. Finnerson himself.

He lowered his eyes, and received a shock. His gaze, instead of encountering a length of neatly striped trousers, rested upon blue serge shorts, a chubby knee, white socks, and a childish shoe. He waggled his foot, and that in the childish shoe responded. Forgetting everything else in this discovery, he looked down his front at a fawn coat with large, flat brass buttons. At the same moment he became aware that he was viewing everything from beneath the curving brim of a yellow straw hat.

The girl gave a sound of impatience. She pushed through the bushes and emerged as a slender figure in a long navy-blue cape. She bent down. A hand, formalized at the wrist by a stiff cuff, emerged from the folds of the cape and fastened upon his upper arm. He was dragged to his feet.

"Come along now," she repeated. "Don't know what's come over you this afternoon, I'm sure."

Clear of the bushes, she shifted her hold to his hand, and called again.

"Barbara. Come along."

Robert tried not to look. Something always cried out in him as if it had been hurt when he looked at Barbara. But in spite of his will his head turned. He saw the little figure in a white frock turn its head, then it came tearing across the grass looking like a large doll. He stared. He had almost forgotten that she had once been like that—as well able to run as any other child—and forgotten, too, what a pretty, happy little thing she had been.

It was quite the most vivid dream he had ever had. Nothing in it was distorted or absurd. The houses sat with an air of respectability around the quiet square. On all four sides they were of a pattern, with variety only in the colors of the spring painting that most of them had received. The composite sounds of life about him were in a pattern, too, that he had forgotten; no rising whine of gears, no revving of engines, no squeal of tires; instead, a background with an utterly different cast blended from the clopping of innumerable hooves, light and heavy, and the creak and rattle of carts. Among it was the jingle of chains and bridles, and somewhere in a nearby street a hurdy-gurdy played a once familiar tune. The beds of tulips had vanished; the wooden seat encircled the old tree as before; the spiked railings stood as he remembered them, stoutly preserving the garden's privacy. He would have liked to pause and taste the flavor of it all again, but that was not permissible.

"Don't drag, now," admonished the voice above him. "We're late for your tea now, and Cook won't like it."

There was a pause while she unlocked the gate and let them out. Then, with their hands in hers, they crossed the road toward a familiar front door, magnificent with new shiny green paint and bright brass knocker. It was a little disconcerting to find that their way in lay by the basement steps and not through this impressive portal.

In the nursery everything was just as it had been, and he stared around him, remembering.

"No time for mooning, if you want your tea," said the voice above.

He went to the table, but he continued to look around, recognizing old friends. The rocking horse with its lower lip missing. The tall wire fire-guard, and the rug in front of it. The three bars across the window. The dado procession of farmyard animals. The gas lamp purring gently above the table. A calendar showing a group of three very woolly kittens, and below, in red and black, the month—May, 1910. Nineteen hundred ten, he reflected; that would mean he was just seven.

At the end of the meal—a somewhat dull meal, perhaps, but doubtless wholesome—Barbara asked:

"Are we going to see Mummy now?"

Nurse shook her head.

"Not now. She's out. So's your daddy. I expect they'll look in at you when they get back—if you're good."

The whole thing was unnaturally clear and detailed: the bathing, the putting to bed. Forgotten things came back to him with an uncanny reality that bemused him. Nurse checked her operations once to look at him searchingly and say:

"Well, you're a quiet one tonight, aren't you? I hope you're not sickening for something."

There was still no fading of the sharp impressions when he lay in bed with only the flickering night light to show the familiar room. The dream was going on for a long time—but then dreams could do that; they could pack a whole sequence into a few seconds. Perhaps this was a special kind of dream, a sort of finale while he sat out there in the garden on that seat: it might be part of the process of dying —the kind of thing people meant when they said, "His whole life flashed before him," only it was a precious slow flash. Quite likely he had overtired himself, after all he was still only convalescent and . . .

At that moment the thought of that clerkly little man, Pendle-something—no, Prendergast—recurred to him. It struck him with such abrupt force that he sat up in bed, looking wildly around. He pinched him-

self—people always did that to make sure they were
awake, though he had never understood why they
should not dream they were pinching themselves. It
certainly felt as if he were awake. He got out of bed
and stood looking about him. The floor was hard and
solid under his feet, the chill in the air quite per-
ceptible, the regular breathing of Barbara, asleep in
her cot, perfectly audible. After a few moments of
bewilderment he got slowly back into bed.

People who wish: "If only I had my life over again."
That was what that fellow Prendergast had said. . . .

Ridiculous . . . utterly absurd, of course—and, anyway, life did not begin at seven years of age—such
a preposterous thing could not happen; it was against
all the laws of Nature. And yet suppose . . . just suppose . . . that once, by some multimillionth chance . . .

Bobby Finnerson lay still, quietly contemplating
an incredible vista of possibilities. He had done pretty
well for himself last time merely by intelligent per-
ception, but now, armed with foreknowledge, what
might he not achieve! In on the ground floor with
radio, plastics, synthetics of all kinds—with pre-
science of the coming wars, of the boom following
the first—*and* of the 1929 slump. Aware of the
trends. Knowing the weapons of the second war before it came, ready for the advent of the atomic age.
Recalling endless oddments of useful information
acquired haphazardly in fifty years. Where was the
catch? Uneasily, he felt sure that there must be a
catch; something to stop him from communicating
or using his knowledge. You couldn't disorganize history, but what was it that could prevent him from
telling, say, the Americans about Pearl Harbor, or

the French about the German plans? There must be something to stop that, but what was it?

There was a theory he had read somewhere—something about parallel universes . . . ?

No. There was just one explanation for it all; in spite of seeming reality, in spite of pinching himself, it was a dream—just a dream . . . or was it?

Some hours later a board creaked outside. The quietly opened door let in a wedge of brighter light from the passage, and then shut it off. Lying still and pretending sleep, he heard careful footsteps approach. He opened his eyes to see his mother bending over him. For some moments he stared unbelievingly at her. She looked lovely in evening dress, with her eyes shining. It was with astonishment that he realized she was still barely more than a girl. She gazed down at him steadily, a little smile around her mouth. He reached up with one hand to touch her smooth cheek. Then, like a piercing bolt, came the recollection of what was going to happen to her. He choked.

She leaned over and gathered him to her, speaking softly not to disturb Barbara.

"There, there, Bobby boy. There's nothing to cry about. Did I wake you suddenly? Was there a horrid dream?"

He snuffled, but said nothing.

"Never mind, darling. Dreams can't hurt you, you know. Just you forget it now, and go to sleep."

She tucked him up, kissed him lightly, and turned to the cot where Barbara lay undisturbed. A minute later she had gone.

Bobby Finnerson lay quiet but awake, gazing up at the ceiling, puzzling, and, tentatively, planning.

The following morning, being a Saturday, involved the formality of going to the morning room to ask for one's pocket money. Bobby was a little shocked by the sight of his father. Not just by the absurd appearance of the tall choking collar and the high-buttoned jacket with mean lapels, but on account of his lack of distinction; he seemed a very much more ordinary young man than he had liked to remember. Uncle George was there, too, apparently as a weekend guest. He greeted Bobby heartily:

"Hullo, young man. By jingo, you've grown since I last saw you. Won't be long before you'll be helping us with the business, at this rate. How'll you like that?"

Bobby did not answer. One could not say: "That won't happen because my father's going to be killed in the war, and you are going to ruin the business through your own stupidity." So he smiled back vaguely at Uncle George, and said nothing at all.

"Do you go to school now?" his uncle added.

Bobby wondered if he did. His father came to the rescue.

"Just a kindergarten in the morning, so far," he explained.

"What do they teach you? Do you know the kings of England?" Uncle George persisted.

"Draw it mild, George," protested Bobby's father. "Did you know 'em when you were just seven—do you now, for that matter?"

"Well, anyway, he knows who's king now, don't you, old man?" asked Uncle George.

Bobby hesitated. He had a nasty feeling that there was a trick about the question, but he had to take a chance.

"Edward the Seventh," he said, and promptly

knew from their faces that it had been the wrong chance.

"I mean, George the Fifth," he amended hastily.

Uncle George nodded.

"Still sounds queer, doesn't it? I suppose they'll be putting G.R. on things soon instead of E.R."

Bobby got away from the room with his Saturday sixpence, and a feeling that it was going to be less easy than he had supposed to act his part correctly.

He had a self-protective determination not to reveal himself until he was pretty sure of his ground, particularly until he had some kind of answer to his chief perplexity: was the knowledge he had that of the things which *must* happen, or was it of those that *ought* to happen? If it was only the former, then he would appear to be restricted to a Cassandra-like role; but if it was the latter, the possibilities were— well, was there any limit?

In the afternoon they were to play in the Square garden. They left the house by the basement door, and he helped the small Barbara with the laborious business of climbing the steps while Nurse turned back for a word with Cook. They walked across the pavement and stood waiting at the curb. The road was empty save for a high-wheeled butcher's trap bowling swiftly toward them. Bobby looked at it, and suddenly a whole horrifying scene jumped back into his memory like a vivid photograph.

He seized his little sister's arm, dragging her back toward the railings. At the same moment he saw the horse shy and begin to bolt. Barbara tripped and fell as it swerved toward them. With frightened strength he tugged her across the pavement. At the area gate he himself stumbled, but he did not let go of her arm. Somehow she fell through the gate after him, and together they rolled down the steps. A second later there was a clash of wild hooves above. A hub ripped into the railings, and slender shiny spokes flew in all directions. A single despairing yell broke from the driver as he flew out of his seat, and then the horse was away with the wreckage bumping and banging behind it, and Sunday joints littering the road.

There was a certain amount of scolding which Bobby took philosophically and forgave because Nurse and the others were all somewhat frightened. His silence covered considerable thought. They did not know, as he did, what *ought* to have happened. He knew how little Barbara *ought* to have been lying on the pavement screaming from the pain of a foot so badly mangled that it would cripple her and so poison the rest of her life. But instead she was just howling healthily from surprise and a few bumps.

That was the answer to one of his questions, and he felt a little shaky as he recognized it. . . .

They put his ensuing "mooniness" down to shock after the narrow escape, and did their best to rally him out of the mood.

Nevertheless, it was still on him at bedtime, for the more he looked at his situation, the more fraught with perplexity it became.

It had, among other things, occurred to him that he could only interfere with another person's life once. Now, for instance, by saving Barbara from that crippling injury, he had entirely altered her future; there was no question of his knowledge interfering with fate's plans for her again, because he had no idea what her new future would be. . . .

That caused him to reconsider the problem of his father's future. If it were to be somehow contrived that he should not be in that particular spot in France, when a shell fell there, he might not be killed at all, and if he wasn't, then the question of preventing his mother from making that disastrous second marriage would never arise. Nor would Uncle George be left single-handed to ruin the business, and if the business wasn't ruined the whole family circumstances would be different. They'd probably send him to a more expensive school, and thus set him on an entirely new course . . . and so on . . . and so on. . . .

Bobby turned restlessly in bed. This wasn't going to be as easy as he had thought . . . it wasn't going to be at all easy. . . .

If his father were to remain alive, there would be a difference at every point where it touched the lives of others, widening like a series of ripples. It might not affect the big things, the pieces of solid history—but something else might. Supposing, for instance, warning were to be given of a certain assassination due to be attempted later at Sarajevo . . . ?

Clearly one must keep well away from the big things. As much as possible one must flow with the previous course of events, taking advantage of them, but being careful always to disrupt them as little as possible. It would be tricky . . . very tricky indeed. . . .

"Prendergast, we have a complaint. A serious complaint over XB2832," announced the Department Director.

"I'm sorry to hear it, sir. I'm sure—"

"Not your fault. It's those Psychiatric fellows again. Get on to them, will you, and give them hell for not making a proper clearance. Tell them the fellow's dislocated one whole ganglion of lives already—and it's lucky it's only a minor ganglion. They'd better get busy, and quickly."

"Very good, sir. I'll get through at once."

Bobby Finnerson awoke, yawned, and sat up in bed. At the back of his mind there was a feeling that this was some special kind of day, like a birthday, or Christmas—only it wasn't really either of those. But it was a day when he had particularly meant to do something. If only he could remember what it was. He looked around the room and at the sunlight pouring in through the window; nothing suggested any specialness. His eyes fell on the cot where Barbara still slept peacefully. He slipped silently out of bed and across the floor. Stealthily he reached out to give a tug at the little plait which lay on the pillow.

It seemed as good as any other way of starting the day.

From time to time as he grew older, that sense of specialness recurred, but he never could find any real explanation for it. In a way it seemed allied with a sensation that would come to him suddenly that he had been in a particular place before, that somehow he knew it already—even though that was not possible. As if life were a little less straightforward and obvious than it seemed. And there were similar sensations, too, flashes of familiarity over something he was doing, a sense felt sometimes, say during a conversation, that it was familiar, almost as though it had all happened before. . . .

It was not a phenomenon confined to his youthful years. During both his early and later middle age it would still unexpectedly occur at times. Just a trick of the mind, they told him. Not even uncommon, they said.

"Prendergast, I see Contract XB2832 is due for renewal again."

"Yes, sir."

"Last time, I recall, there was some little technical trouble. It might be as well to remind the Psychiatric Department in advance."

"Very good, sir."

Robert Finnerson lay dying. Two or three times before he had been under the impression that he might be dying. He had been frightened. . . .

Beyond the Game

BY VANCE AANDAHL

*The things people do to each other in the name
of sport are hard to believe. What is more likely
to be a reality, after all—that boys should vi-
ciously hurt each other in "games," or that
bears might wrestle in the sun?*

Dry and white as chalk in his gym shorts,
Ernest crouched under the fat red backs of Balfe and
Basil Basset and shivered as the naked bumps of his
spine brushed against the wall behind him. He knew
from previous games that the twins would be too hys-
terical to run; for a while, at least, he could hide
safely behind them. His fingers trilled against his
cheeks.

Staring through the narrow space between Balfe's
soft thighs, he could see the boys of the enemy team
lined against the far wall. All of them looked tall and
lean and hungry for the game; some strutted in
place; others contorted their mouths into ravenous
grins and shouted threats across the gym. Hunker-
ing down, Ernest laced his slender arms around his
slender legs and kissed his knees. His eyes moved to
the teacher.

Miss Argentine paused halfway between the two

teams and adjusted the canvas bag that dangled from her shoulder like an enormous cocoon. She was walking along the black line that halved the gym, bending after every step to take a ball from the bag and place it on the line. Ernest gazed at the balls. There were basketballs with pebbled rubber skins and footballs of rough leather, smooth white volleyballs that spun when you threw them and furry gray tennis balls that stung when they hit, mushy softballs with peeling cases and hard little handballs of solid rubber.

The rules of the game were very simple, and even Ernest knew them. Each team had to stay in its own half of the gym; no one could cross the center line. If someone on the other team hit you with a ball, you were eliminated and had to stand against the side wall; but if you caught the ball without dropping it, then he was eliminated instead. If the ball missed you completely and hit the floor or a wall, then nobody was eliminated. Only when one team had completely wiped out the other did the game end, and rarely were there more than three or four survivors on the winning side.

Miss Argentine set the last ball on the line and retreated to stand with her shoulders against the side wall. An absolute silence filled the gym. She turned her head and looked at Ernest's team. Her face was the color of clouded silver. Her eyes looked like sandpapered zinc. When she spotted Ernest behind the Basset twins, a smile slowly split the stark plane between her nose and jaw, and she lifted a green tin whistle to her mouth and rolled it for a moment on the tip of her tongue. Then her lips hardened.

Suddenly the silence was pierced by the shrill of her whistle.

As Balfe and Basil squeaked and gibbered with excitement, Ernest huddled beneath their ponderous buttocks and watched the game begin. At the sound of the whistle, boys on each team had charged recklessly for the center line. Sprinting hard and fast from the opposite wall, Freddy Guymon and Jim Genz had reached the balls before anyone on Ernest's team was even close. Freddy hit Bobby Graffigna in the knees with a basketball, and Jim hit Ben Lee in the neck with a tennis ball, Gerald Francis in the thigh with a softball, and Rae Stalker in the chest with another softball. The other boys on Ernest's team scrambled back to their wall.

Hooting and yelping their derision, the entire enemy team crowded up to the center line to collect the rest of the balls. They jumped up and down like the naked savages that Ernest conjured up in the dark rain forests of his mind.

"All right, you guys!" Jim Genz lifted a football in his right hand and shook it above his head. "Get ready! Get set! *Give it to 'em!*"

The air thickened with balls. Cowering back against the wall, Ernest watched them in a dream of soft terror; they grew larger and larger as they skirred toward them at incredible speeds, and he could see the dark-brown laces on the footballs, the white stitching on the softballs. The horror of waiting seemed to last forever. Then he suddenly realized that it was over and he hadn't been hit.

Balfe turned slowly to face Ernest. Both of his hands were clamped over his forehead. Two tears slid from the corner of his left eye and rolled across his cheek; another tear fell from his left nostril and splattered on his lips; then his mouth crinkled into fluted piecrust, and he began to sputter and whine and bawl. It must have been one of the handballs; they were hard as ice. His forehead would have a purple welt for days.

"Run, Balfe! Get over to the side wall before she sees you!" Basil shoved his brother frantically. His cheeks reddening with pain, his shoulders shaking with sobs, Balfe waddled away to join the others who had been eliminated.

A ball hurtled against the wall next to Ernest's ear, and he jerked his eyes away from Balfe to stare across the gym. His own team had just barraged the enemy with nine or ten balls, and now snipers on both sides were edging up the sidelines. Loose balls bounced and dribbled and rolled in every direction. Screams of triumph mingled with shrieks of anger. Two basketballs collided in midair and bounded through a spray of tennis balls. Ernest curled himself into a tiny knot of flesh, half protected by Basil's calves, and retreated into dazed abstraction: high on the wall above Miss Argentine, the heavy wire mesh that protected the gym's single window was rattling on its loosened screws, and beyond it, distorted by the vibrating glass in the panes, a single updrift of green smoke wavered once, then billowed, then melted into the smog that hung in thick gray curtains over the city. And what color was the sky beyond the smog? Ernest's teachers had said it was blue, but even now he could see tiny diamond-winged angels diving from banks of pearl into the golden rivers of the sun. . . .

"Ooooooooo . . ."

Basil swayed and sank to one knee. Then he lay over on his side and clutched his groin with both hands. His pudgy fingers fluttered like birds.

"Ooooooooo . . ."

Defenseless and exposed, Ernest staggered to his feet and skittered back and forth against the wall, looking for someone to hide behind. But everyone was running now, rushing madly forward to throw a ball, leaping desperately back to duck another, dashing and darting and diving in helter-skelter, skimble-skamble confusion. His head ached from the roar of their voices; his vision spun into a blurred pinwheel of skin and leather, wood and plaster. At last he crouched down in a corner with his back to the game. He squeezed shut his eyes, screwed the butts of his thumbs into his ears to dampen the clamor, and waited in a buzzing trance for a ball to hit his back. He hoped only that it would be a volleyball or a tennis ball, not a handball.

And then he saw a slender boy running naked down the grassy slopes, trotting past the palm trees cottony with spiderwebs, jogging into a thicket of emerald ferns and gray sawtooth reeds and nodding white lotus blossoms, and presently he knew that he wasn't just watching the boy, knew that he was the boy himself, that he was actually there, sprawling with arms and legs akimbo beneath a luxurious profusion of chocolate and saffron flowers, panting quickly at the hot pulsing heart of the sun in a sky as white and grainy as the warm sand beneath his shoulders, crawling finally into the zebra-stripe shadows to wait for the bears . . . and the bears *did* come, lurched one by one out of their secret tunnels into the blinding sunlight, stumbled by giddy threes and fours down to the river shallows, munched the tubers that grew there beneath the water, splashed each other with glassy pawfuls of river, then fell to indolent wrestling in the golden mud—black bears and brown bears, cinnamon bears and honey bears, regal Kodiaks and surly grizzlies, even a family of great white polar bears, their paws batting in bewildered discomfort at the steaming heat of the jungle, their eyes glittering like melting snow-crust. . . .

Suddenly Ernest realized that he was wrapped in complete silence. He took his hands away from his ears. The silence persisted, deepened.

Opening his eyes, he turned slowly on his knees and blinked across the gym. They were standing against the side wall—every one of them—and they were all staring at him.

Covering his mouth with his hands, he lifted himself into half a stance and gazed shamefully down at the litter of balls on the floor. How could it have happened? His fingers grew cold as stones against his lips.

No one moved; no one smiled. He prayed desperately for disappearance, for death.

"Look at the pee-wee." Miss Argentine's voice clipped through the silence like a rusty tin-snip. "Hims doesn't want to play. Hims is *frightened.*"

No one laughed.

"But hims will just have to *learn* how to play, won't hims?"

Ernest's cheeks prickled with heat. He tried to take his hands away from his mouth, but he couldn't; he tried to look up at Miss Argentine, but he couldn't.

"All right, the rest of you go stand at the other end of the gym. We're going to play one more game. Yes, *all* of you, at *that* end of the gym, *right* now."

Ernest felt nauseous. The entire class was lining up at the far end of the gym; there were so many of them that they had to stand two deep.

He sank to his knees. He could hear the sharp click of her heels as she walked back and forth across the floor. She was picking up the scattered balls and rearranging them along the center line.

He knew then that it couldn't really be happening. It was only a nightmare, only an illusion.

"Is the pee-wee ready? This time hims *has* to play, doesn't hims?"

He finally forced himself to lift his head. She was standing at her customary post against the side wall. Her face was still the color of clouded silver—and her eyes were still as flat and dead as sandpapered zinc. The corners of her mouth curled up into her cheeks, not in a smile, not in an ordinary smile, but rather in a pathic grimace of lust.

Then she lifted the green tin whistle to her lips.

But Ernest wasn't watching her anymore. He broke through the contorted metal cage of her face and burned a fiery furrow up the wall and melted the heavy wire mesh and seared through the window in a hiss of smoking glass . . . and suddenly he was far beyond Miss Argentine, far beyond the horrors of the gym, far beyond the thick curtains of smog that hung forever motionless over the city, far beyond the trivial shadows of his nightmare.

He never heard the whistle.

He was swimming in a sea of stars . . .

Touchstone

BY TERRY CARR

> touchstone (*tuch ston*), n. *1*. Mineral. *A black, siliceous stone allied to flint;—used to test the purity of gold and silver by the streak left on the stone when rubbed by the metal. 2. Any test or criterion by which to try a thing's qualities.*

That's the dictionary definition of one kind of touchstone. The more common kind today is a feeling piece such as the one described in this story. But both definitions apply, yes.

$\mathcal{F}$*or thirty-two years,* during which he watched with growing perplexity and horror the ways of the world and the dull gropings of men reaching for love and security, Randolph Helgar had told himself that there was a simple answer to all of it—somehow it was possible to get a handhold on life, to hold it close and cherish it without fear. And on a Saturday morning in early March when the clouds had disappeared and the sun came forth pale in the sky he found what he had been looking for.

The snow had been gone from the streets of Greenwich Village for over a week, leaving behind only the crispness on the sidewalks. Everyone still walked with a tentative step, like sailors on shore leave. Randolph Helgar was out of his apartment by ten, heading west. His straight, sandy hair was ruffled by an easterly wind, giving him the superficial appearance of hurrying, but his quick gray eyes and the faint smile that so often came to his mouth dispelled that. Randolph was busier looking around than walking.

The best thing about the Village, as far as he was concerned, was that you could never chart all of it. As soon as you thought you knew every street, every sandal shop, every hot dog or pizza stand, one day you'd look up and there'd be something new there, where you'd never looked before. A peculiar blindness comes over people who walk through the streets of the Village; they see only where they're going.

The day before, on the bus coming home from work at the travel agency on West Fourth, he had looked out the window and seen a bookstore whose dirty windows calmly testified to the length of time it had been there. So of course this morning he was looking for that bookstore. He had written down the address, but there was no need now for him to take the slip of paper from his wallet to look at it; the act of writing it had fixed it in his memory.

The store was just opening when he got there. A large, heavy-shouldered man with thick black hair and prominent veins in the backs of his hands was setting out the bargain table in the front of the store. Randolph glanced at the table, filled with the sun-faded spines of anonymous pocketbooks, and nodded at the man. He went inside.

The books were piled high around the walls; here

and there were hand-lettered signs saying MUSIC, HISTORY, PSYCHOLOGY, but they must have been put there years ago, because the books in those sections bore no relation to the signs. Near the front was an old cupboard, mottled with the light that came through the dirty window; a sign on one of its shelves said *$10*. Next to it was a small round table which revolved on its base, but there was no price on this.

The owner had come back into the store now, and he stood just inside the door looking at Randolph. After a moment he said, "You want anything special?"

Randolph shook his head, dislodging the shock of hair which fell over his eyes. He ran his fingers through it, combing it back, and turned to one of the piles of books.

"I think maybe you'd be interested in this section," said the owner, walking heavily over the bending floorboards to stand beside Randolph. He raised a large hand and ran it along one shelf. A sign said MAGIC, WITCHCRAFT.

Randolph glanced at it. "No," he said.

"None of those books are for sale," the man said. "That section is strictly lending-library."

Randolph raised his eyes to meet those of the older man. The man gazed back calmly, waiting.

"Not for sale?" Randolph said.

"No, they're part of my own collection," the man said. "But I lend them out at ten cents a day, if anybody wants to read them, or . . ."

"Who takes them out?"

The heavy man shrugged, with the faint touch of a smile about his thick lips. "People. People come in, they see the books and think they might like to read them. They always bring them back."

Randolph glanced at the books on the shelves. The spines were crisp and hard, the lettering on them like new. "Do you think they read them?" he asked.

"Of course. So many of them come back and buy other things."

"Other books?"

The man shrugged again, and turned away. He walked slowly to the back of the store. "I sell other things. It's impossible to make a living selling books in this day and age."

Randolph followed him into the darkness in back. "What other things do you sell?"

"Perhaps you should read some of the books first," the man said, watching him beneath his eyebrows.

"Do you sell . . . love potions? Dried bat's blood? Snake's entrails?"

"No," said the man. "I'm afraid you'd have to search the tobacconist's shops for such things as that. I sell only imperishables."

"Magic charms?" Randolph said.

"Yes," the man said slowly. "Some are real, some are not."

"And I suppose the real ones are more expensive."

"They are all roughly the same price. It's up to you to decide which ones are real."

The man had stooped to reach into a drawer of his desk, and now he brought out a box from which he lifted the lid. He set the open box on the top of his desk and reached up to turn on a naked light bulb which hung from the shadowed ceiling.

The box contained an assortment of amulets, stones, dried insects encased in glass, carved pieces of wood, and other things. They were all tumbled into the box haphazardly. Randolph stirred the contents with two fingers.

"I don't believe in magic," he said.

The heavy man smiled faintly. "I don't suppose I do either. But some of these things are quite interesting. Some are of authentic South American workmanship, and others are from Europe and the East. They're worth money, all right."

"What's this?" Randolph asked, picking up a black stone that just fitted into the palm of his hand. The configurations of the stone twisted around and in upon themselves, like a lump of baker's dough.

"That's a touchstone. Run your fingers over it."

"It's perfectly smooth," Randolph said.

"It's supposed to have magical powers to make people feel contented. Hold it in your hand."

Randolph closed his fingers around the stone. Perhaps it was the power of suggestion, but the stone did feel very good. So smooth, like skin. . . .

"The man who gave it to me said it was an ancient Indian piece. It embodies yin and yang, the opposites that complement and give harmony to the world. You can see a little of the symbol in the way the stone looks." He smiled slowly. "It's also supposed to encase a human soul, like an egg."

"More likely a fossil," Randolph said. He wondered what kind of stone it was.

"It will cost five dollars," the man said.

Randolph hefted the stone in his hand. It settled back into his palm comfortably, like a cat going to sleep. "All right," he said.

He took a bill from his wallet, and noticed the paper on which he'd written the store's address the day before. "If I come back here a week from now," he said, "will this store still be here? Or will it have disappeared, like magic shops are supposed to do?"

The man didn't smile. "This isn't that kind of store. I'd go out of business if I kept moving my location."

"Well then," Randolph said, looking at the black stone in his hand. "When I was young I used to pick up stones at the beach and carry them around for weeks, just because I loved them. I suppose this stone has some of that sort of magic, anyway."

"If you decide you don't want it, bring it back," said the man.

When he got back to the apartment, Margo was just getting up. Bobby, seven years old, was apparently up and out already. Randolph put yesterday's pot of coffee on the burner to heat and sat at the kitchen table to wait for it. He took the touchstone out of his pocket and ran his fingers over it.

Strange. . . . It was just a black rock, worn smooth probably by water and then maybe by the rubbing of fingers over centuries. Despite what the man at the store had said about an Indian symbol, it had no particular shape.

Yet it did have a peculiar calming effect on him. Maybe, he thought, it's just that people have to have something to do with their hands while they think. It's the hands, the opposable thumb, that has made men what they are, or so the anthropologists say. The hands give men the ability to work with things around them, to make, to do. And we all have a feeling that we've got to be using our hands all the time or somehow we're not living up to our birthright.

That's why so many people smoke. That's why they fidget and rub their chins and drum their fingers on tables. But the touchstone relaxes the hands.

A simple form of magic.

Margo came into the kitchen, combing her long hair back over her shoulders. She hadn't put on any makeup, and her full mouth seemed as pale as clouds. She set out coffee cups and poured, then sat down across the table.

"Did you get the paint?"

"Paint?"

"You were going to paint the kitchen today. The old paint is cracking and falling off."

Randolph looked up at the walls, rubbing the stone in his fingers. They didn't look bad, he decided. They could go for another six months without being re-done. After all, it was no calamity if the plaster showed through above the stove.

"I don't think I'll do it today," he said.

Margo didn't say anything. She picked up a book from the chair beside her and found her place in it.

Randolph fingered the touchstone and thought about the beach when he had been a boy.

There was a party that night at Gene Blake's apartment on the floor below, but for once Randolph didn't feel like going down. Blake was four years younger than he, and suddenly today the difference seemed insuperable; Blake told off-center jokes about integration in the South, talked about writers Randolph knew only by the reviews in the Sunday *Times*, and was given to drinking Scotch and milk. No, not tonight, he told Margo.

After dinner Randolph settled in front of the television set and, as the washing dishes sounded from the kitchen and Bobby read a comic book in the corner, watched a rerun of the top comedy show of three seasons past. When the second commercial came on he dug the touchstone from his pocket and rubbed it idly with his thumb. All it takes, he told himself, is to ignore the commercials.

"Have you ever seen a frog?" Bobby asked him. He looked up and saw the boy standing next to his chair, breathing quickly as boys do when they have something to say.

"Sure," he said.

"Did you ever see a black one? A dead one?"

Randolph thought a minute. He didn't suppose he had. "No," he said.

"Wait a minute!" Bobby said, and bounded out of the room. Randolph turned back to the television screen, and saw that the wife had a horse in the living room and was trying to coax it to go upstairs before the husband came home. The horse seemed bored.

"Here!" said Bobby, and dropped the dead frog in his lap.

Randolph looked at it for two seconds before he realized what it was. One leg and part of the frog's side had been crushed, probably by a car's wheel, and the wide mouth was open. It was gray, not black.

Randolph shook it off him onto the floor. "You'd better throw it away," he said. "It's going to smell bad."

"But I paid sixty marbles for him!" Bobby said. "And I only had twenty-five, and you got to get me some more."

Randolph sighed, and shifted the touchstone from one hand to the other. "All right," he said. "Monday. Keep him in your room."

He turned back to the screen, where everyone had got behind the horse and was trying to push him up the stairs.

"Don't you like him?" Bobby asked.

Randolph looked blankly at him.

"My frog," Bobby said.

Randolph thought about it for a moment. "I think you'd better throw him away," he said. "He's going to stink."

Bobby's face fell. "Can I ask Mom?"

Randolph didn't answer, and he supposed Bobby went away. There was another commercial on now, and he was toying idly with the thought of a commercial for touchstones. "For two thousand years mankind has searched for the answer to underarm odor, halitosis, regularity. Now at last . . ."

"*Bobby!*" said his wife in the kitchen. Randolph looked up, surprised. "Take that out in the hall and put it in the garbage *right now!* Not another word!"

In a moment Bobby came trudging through the room, his chin on his chest. But sad eyes looked at Randolph with a trace of hope.

"She's gonna make me throw him away."

Randolph shrugged. "It would smell up the place," he said.

"Well, I thought *you'd* like it anyway," Bobby said. "You always keep telling me how *you* were a boy, and *she* wasn't." He stopped for a moment, waiting for Randolph to answer, and when he didn't, the boy abruptly ran out with the gray crushed frog in his hand.

Margo came into the living room, drying her hands on a towel. "Ran, why didn't you put your foot down in the first place?"

"What?"

"You know things like that make me sick. I won't be able to eat for two days."

"I was watching the program," he said.

"You've seen that one twice before. What's the matter with you?"

"Take some aspirin if you're upset," he said. He squeezed the stone in the palm of his hand until she shook her head and went away.

A few minutes later a news program came on with a report on some people who had picketed a military base, protesting bombs and fallout. A university professor's face came on the screen and gravely he pointed to a chart. "The Atomic Energy Commission admits—"

Randolph sighed and shut the set off.

He went to bed early that night. When he woke up the next day he went and got a book and brought it back to bed with him. He picked up the touchstone from the chair next to the bed and turned it over in his hand a few times. It was really a very plain kind of stone. Black, smooth, softly curving. . . . What was it about the rock that could make everything seem so unimportant, so commonplace?

Well, of course a rock is one of the most common things in the world, he thought. You find them everywhere—even in the streets of the city, where everything is man-made, you'll find rocks. They're part of the ground underneath the pavement, part of the world we live on. They're part of home.

He held the touchstone in one hand while he read.

Margo had been up for several hours when he finished the book. When he set it down she came in and stood in the doorway, watching him silently.

After a few minutes she asked, "Do you love me?"

He looked up, faintly surprised. "Yes, of course."

"I wasn't sure."

"Why not? Is anything wrong?"

She came over and sat on the bed next to him in her terry-cloth robe. "It's just that you've hardly spoken to me since yesterday. I thought maybe you were angry about something."

Randolph smiled. "No. Why should I be angry?"

"I don't know. It just seemed that . . ." She shrugged.

He reached out and touched her face with his free hand. "Don't worry about it."

She lay down beside him, resting her head on his arm. "And you do love me? Everything's all right?"

He turned the stone over in his right hand. "Of course everything's all right," he said softly.

She pressed against him. "I want to kiss you."

"All right." He turned to her and brushed his lips across her forehead and nose. Then she held him tightly while she kissed his mouth.

When she had finished he lay back against the pillow and looked up at the ceiling. "Is it sunny out today?" he asked. "It's been dark in here all day."

"I want to kiss you some more," she said. "If that's all right with you."

Randolph was noticing the warmth of the touchstone in his hand. Rocks aren't warm, he thought; it's only my hand that gives it warmth. Strange.

"Of course it's all right," he said, and turned to let her kiss him again.

Bobby stayed in his room most of the day; Randolph supposed he was doing something. Margo, after that one time, didn't try to talk to him. Randolph stayed in bed fingering the touchstone and thinking, though whenever he tried to remember what he'd been thinking about he drew a blank.

Around five-thirty his friend Blake appeared at the door. Randolph heard him say something to Margo, and then he came into the bedroom.

"Hey, are you all right? You weren't at the party last night."

Randolph shrugged. "Sure, I just felt like lounging around this weekend."

Blake's weathered face cleared. "Well, that's good. Listen, I've got a problem."

"A problem," Randolph said. He settled down in the bed, looking idly at the stone in his hand.

Blake paused. "You sure everything's all right? Nothing wrong with Margo? She didn't look too good when I came in."

"We're both fine."

"Well, okay. Look, Ran, you know you're the only close friend I've got, don't you? I mean, there's a lot of people in the world, but you're the only one I can really count on when the chips are down. Some people I joke with, but with you I can talk. You listen. You know?"

Randolph nodded. He supposed Blake was right.

"Well . . . I guess you heard the commotion last night. A couple guys drank too much, and there was a fight."

"I went to bed early."

"I'm surprised you slept through it. It developed into quite a brawl for a while; the cops came later on. They broke three windows and somebody pushed over the refrigerator. Smashed everything all to hell. One of the doors is off the hinges."

"No, I didn't hear it."

"Wow. Well, look, Ran . . . the super is on my neck. He's going to sue me, he's going to kick me out. You know that guy. I've got to get hold of some money fast, to fix things up."

Randolph didn't say anything. He had found a place on the stone where his right thumb fit perfectly, as though the stone had been molded around it. He switched the stone to his left hand, but it didn't quite fit that thumb.

Blake was nervous. "Look, I know it's short notice. I wouldn't ask you, but I'm stuck. Can you lend me about a hundred?"

"A hundred dollars?"

"I might be able to get by with eighty, but I figured a bribe to the super . . ."

"All right. It doesn't make any difference."

Blake paused again, looking at him. "You can do it?"

"Sure."

"Which—eighty or a hundred?"

"A hundred if you want."

"You're sure it won't . . . bother you, make you short? I mean, I could look around somewhere else. . . ."

"I'll write you a check," Randolph said. He got up slowly and took his checkbook from the dresser. "How do you spell your first name?"

"G-e-n-e." Blake stood nervously, indecisive. "You're sure it's no trouble? I don't want to pressure you."

"No." Randolph signed the check, tore it out and handed it to him.

"You're a friend," Blake said. "A real one."

Randolph shrugged. "What the hell."

Blake stood for a few seconds more, apparently wanting to say something. But then he thanked him again and hurried out. Margo came and stood in the doorway and looked at him silently for a moment, then went away.

"Are you going to get me the marbles tomorrow?" Bobby said that evening over supper.

"Marbles?"

"I told you. I still have to pay that guy for the frog you made me throw away."

"Oh. How many?"

"Thirty-five of them. I owed him sixty, and I only had twenty-five."

Bobby was silent, picking at his corn. He speared three kernels carefully with his fork and slid them off the fork with his teeth.

"I'll bet you forget."

Margo looked up from where she had been silently eating. "Bobby!"

"I'm finished with my dinner," Bobby said quickly, standing up. He threw a quick glance at Randolph. "I'll bet he does forget," he said, and ran out.

When the telephone rang in the morning he came out of sleep slowly. It was ringing for the fifth time when he answered it.

It was Howard, at the agency. "Are you all right?" he asked.

"Yes, I'm all right," Randolph said.

"It's past ten. We thought maybe you were sick and couldn't call."

"Past ten?" For a moment he didn't know what

that meant. Then Margo appeared in the doorway from the kitchen, holding the alarm clock in her hand, and he remembered it was Monday.

"I'll be there in an hour or so," he said quickly. "It's all right; Margo wasn't feeling too good, but she's all right now."

Margo, her face expressionless, put the clock down on the chair next to the bed and looked at him for a moment before leaving the room.

"Nothing serious, I hope," said Howard.

"No, it's all right. I'll see you in a while." He hung up.

He sat on the edge of the bed and tried to remember what had happened. The past two days were a blur. He had lost something, hadn't he? Something he'd been holding.

"I tried to wake you three times," Margo said quietly. She had come back into the room and was standing with her hands folded under her breasts. Her voice was level, controlled. "But you wouldn't pay any attention."

Randolph was slowly remembering. He'd had the touchstone in his hand last night, but it must have slipped out while he was asleep. He began to search among the covers.

"Did you see the stone?" he asked her.

"What?"

"The stone. I've dropped it."

There was a short silence. "I don't know. Is it so important right now?"

"I paid five dollars for it," he said, still rummaging through the bed.

"For a rock?"

He stopped suddenly. Yes, five dollars for a rock, he thought. It didn't sound right.

"Ran, what's the matter with you lately? Gene Blake was up here this morning. He gave back your check and said to apologize to you. He was really upset. He said he didn't think you really wanted to loan him the money."

But it wasn't just a rock, Randolph thought. It was a black, smooth touchstone.

"Is something worrying you?" she asked him.

The back of his neck was suddenly cold. Worrying me? he thought. No, nothing's been worrying me. That's just the trouble.

He looked up. "It may be cold out today. Can you find my gloves?"

She looked at him for a moment and then went to the hall closet. Randolph got up and started dressing. In a few minutes she returned with the gloves. He put them on. "It's a little cold in here right now," he said.

When she had gone back into the kitchen he started looking through the bed again, this time coldly and carefully. He found the touchstone under his pillow, and without looking at it he slipped it into a paper bag. He put the bag into his coat pocket.

When he got to the agency he made his excuses as glibly as possible, but he was sure they all knew that he had simply overslept. Well, it wasn't that important . . . once.

He stopped off at the store on his way home that night. It was just as he remembered it, and the same man was inside. He raised his thick eyebrows when he saw Randolph.

"You came back quickly."

"I want to return the touchstone," Randolph said.

"I'm not surprised. So many people return my magic pieces. Sometimes I think I am only lending them too, like the books."

"Will you buy it back?"

"Not at the full price. I have to stay in business."

"What price?" Randolph asked.

"A dollar only," the man said. "Or you could keep it, if that's not enough."

Randolph thought for a moment. He certainly didn't intend to keep the stone, but a dollar wasn't much. He could throw the stone away. . . .

But then someone would probably pick it up.

"Do you have a hammer here?" he asked. "I think it would be better to break the stone."

"Of course I have a hammer," the man said. He reached into one of the lower drawers of his desk and brought one out, old and brown with rust.

He held it out. "The hammer rents for a dollar," he said.

Randolph glanced sharply at the man, and then decided that that wasn't really surprising. He had to stay in business, yes. "All right." He took the hammer. "I wonder if the veins of the rock are as smooth as the outside."

"Perhaps we'll see the fossilized soul," said the man. "I never know about the things I sell."

Randolph knelt and dropped the touchstone from its bag onto the floor. It rolled in a wobbling circle and then lay still.

"I knew quite a bit about rocks when I was young," he said. "I used to pick them up at the beach."

He brought the hammer down on the touchstone

and it shattered into three pieces which skittered across the floor and bounced to a stop. The largest one was next to Randolph's foot.

He picked it up and the owner of the store turned on the overhead light bulb. Together they examined the rock's fragment.

There was a fossil, but Randolph couldn't tell what it was. It was small and not very distinct, but looking at it he felt a chill strike out at him. It was as ugly and unformed as a human fetus, but it was something older, a kind of life that had died in the world's mud before anything like a man had been born.

Are You Listening?

BY HARLAN ELLISON

Ever get the feeling people are ignoring you, that they don't listen to what you say or even care that you exist? Well, maybe you don't exist. At least, as far as other people can tell— maybe you've completely faded out of their perceptions. Harlan Ellison (the last person you'd ever expect to have suffered from such a problem) tells of a man who discovered one day that he'd disappeared . . . and what he did about it.

There are several ways I wanted to start telling this. First, I was going to begin it:

I began to lose my existence on a Tuesday morning. . . .

But then I thought about it and:

This is my horror story.

. . . seemed like a better way to begin. But after thinking it over (I've had a devil of a lot of time to think it over, believe you me), I realized both of those were pretty melodramatic, and if I wanted to instill trust and faith and all that from the outset, I had just better begin the way it happened, and tell it through to now, and then make my offer and, well, let you decide for yourself.

Are you listening?

Perhaps it all began with my genes. Or my chromosomes. Whichever or whatever combination made me a Casper Milquetoast prototype, that or those are to blame, I'm sure. I woke up a year ago on a Tuesday morning in March and knew I was the same as I had been for hundreds of other mornings past. I was forty-seven years old; I was balding; my eyes were good—and the glasses I used only for reading. I slept in a separate room from my wife, Alma, and I wore long underwear—chiefly because I've always picked up a chill quickly.

The only thing that might possibly be considered out-of-the-ordinary about me is that my name is Winsocki.

Albert Winsocki.

You know, like the song . . . "Buckle down, Winsocki, you can win, Winsocki, if you'll only buckle down. . . ." Very early in life I was teased about that, but my mild nature kept me from taking offense, and instead of growing to loathe it, I adopted it as a sort of personal anthem. Whenever I find myself whistling something, it is usually that.

However—

I woke up that morning, and got dressed quickly. It was too cold to take a shower, so I just dabbed water on my wrists and face, and dressed quickly. As I started down the stairs, Zasu, my wife's Persian, swept past between my legs. Zasu is a pretty stable cat, and I had never been quite snubbed before, though the animal *had* taken to ignoring me with great skill. But this morning of which I speak, she just swarmed past with not even a *meowrll* or a spit. It was unusual, but not remarkable.

But just an indication of what was to come.

I came into the living room, and saw that Alma had laid out my paper on the arm of the sofa, just as she had done for twenty-seven years. I picked it up in passing and came into the dinette.

My orange juice was set out, and I could hear Alma in the kitchen beyond. She was muttering to herself, as usual. That is one of my wife's unpleasant habits, I'm afraid. At heart she is a sweet, dear woman, but when she gets annoyed, she murmurs. Nothing obscene, for goodness' sake, but just at the bare threshold of audibility, so that it niggles and naggles and bothers. She *knew* it bothered me, or perhaps she didn't, I'm not sure. I don't think Alma was aware that I really *had* any likes or dislikes of any real strength.

At any rate, there she was, muttering and murmuring, so I just called out, "I'm down, dear. Good morning." Then I turned to the paper and the juice.

The paper was full of the same sort of stuff, and what else could orange juice be but orange juice?

However, as the minutes passed, Alma's mutters did not pass away. In fact, they got louder, more angry, more annoyed. "Where *is* that man? He *knows* I despise waiting breakfast! Now look . . . the eggs are hard. Oh, where *is* he?"

This kept up for some time, though I repeatedly yelled in to her, "Alma, *please* stop, I'm here. I'm down, can't you understand?"

Finally, she came storming past and went through into the living room. I could hear her at the foot of the stairs—hand on banister, one foot up on the first step—yelling up to no one at all, "Albert! *Will* you come down? Are you in the bathroom again? Are you having trouble with your kidneys? Shall I come up?"

Well, that was too much, so I laid aside my napkin and got up. I walked up behind her and said, just as politely as I could, "Alma. What is the matter with you, dear? I'm right here."

It made no impression.

She continued howling, and a few moments later stalked upstairs. I sat down on the steps, because I was sure Alma had lost her mind or her hearing had gone or something. After twenty-seven happily married years, my wife was dreadfully ill.

I didn't know what to do. I was totally at a loss. I decided it would be best to call Dr. Hairshaw. So I went over and dialed him, and his phone rang three times before he picked it up and said, "Hello?"

I always felt guilty calling him, no matter what time of the day it was—he had *such* an intimidating tone—but I felt even *more* self-conscious this time, because there was a decidedly muggy value to his voice. As though he had just gotten out of bed.

"Sorry to wake you at this hour, Doctor," I said quickly. "This is Albert Winso—"

He cut me off with, "Hello? Hello?"

I repeated, "Hello, Doctor? This is Al—"

"Hello there? Anyone there?"

I didn't know what to say. It was probably a bad connection, so I screamed as loud as I could. "Doctor, this is—"

"Oh, *hell!* he yelled, and jammed down the receiver.

I stood there for a second with the handpiece gripped tightly, and I'm dreadfully afraid an expression of utter bewilderment came over my face. Had everyone gone deaf today? I was about to redial when Alma came down the stairs, talking out loud to herself.

"Now *where* on earth can that man have gone? Don't tell me he got up and went out without any breakfast? Oh, well, that's less work for today."

And she went right smack past me staring right *through* me, and into the kitchen. I plunked down the receiver and started after her. This was *too* much! During the past few years Alma had lessened her attentions to me, even at times seemed to ignore me; I would speak and she would not hear; I would touch her and she would not respond. There had been increasingly more of these occasions, but this was too much!

I went into the kitchen and walked up behind her. She did not turn, just continued scouring the eggs out of the pan with steel wool. I screamed her name. She did not turn, did not even break the chain of humming.

I grabbed the pan from her hands and banged it as hard as I could on the stove top (something remarkably violent for me, but I'm sure you can understand that this was a remarkable situation). She did not even start at the noise. She went over to the icebox and took out the cube trays. She began to defrost the box.

That was the last straw. I slammed the pan to the floor and stalked out of the room. I was on the verge of swearing, I was so mad. What kind of game *was* this? All right, so she didn't want to make my breakfast; so that was just one more little ignoring factor I had to put up with. All right, so why didn't she just say so? But this folderol was too much!

I put on my hat and coat and left the house—slamming the door as hard as I could.

I glanced at my pocket watch and saw the time

had long since passed for me to catch my bus to the office. I decided to take a taxi, though I wasn't quite sure my budget could afford the added strain. But it was a necessity, so I walked past the bus stop and hailed a cab as it went past. Went past is correct. It zipped by me without even slowing. I had seen it was empty, so why didn't the cabbie stop? Had he been going off duty? I supposed that was it, but after eight others had whizzed by, I was certain something was wrong.

But I could not discern what the trouble might be. I decided, since I saw it coming, to take the bus anyhow. A young girl in a tight skirt and funny little hat was now waiting at the stop, and I looked at her rather sheepishly, saying, "I just can't figure out these cabmen, can you?"

She ignored me. I mean, she didn't turn away as she would to some masher, nor did she give me a cursory glance and not reply. I mean, she didn't know I was there.

I didn't have any more time to think about it, because the bus stopped and the girl got on. I started up the steps and barely made it, for the bus driver slammed the doors with a wheeze, catching the tail of my coat.

"Hey! I'm caught!" I yelled, but he paid no attention. He watched in his rear-view mirror as the girl walked swayingly to her seat. The bus was crowded and I didn't want to make a fool of myself, so I reached out and pulled his pants leg. Still, he didn't respond.

That was when the idea started to form.

I yanked my coattail loose, and I was so mad I decided to make him *ask* for his fare. I walked back, expecting any moment to hear him say, "Hey, you, mister. You forgot to pay your fare." Then I was going to respond, "I'll pay my fare, but I'll report you to your company, too!"

But even that tiny bit of satisfaction was denied me, because he continued to drive, and his head did not turn. I think that made me angrier than if he had insulted me; what the hell was going on? Oh, excuse me, but that was what I was thinking, and I hope you'll pardon the profanity, but I want to get this across just as it happened.

Are you listening?

Though I shoved between an apoplectic man in a Tyrolean hat and a gaggle of high school girls when disembarking, though I nudged and elbowed and shoved them, just desperately *fighting* to be recognized, no one paid me the slightest heed. I even—I'm so ashamed now that I think of it—I slapped one of the girls on her, uh, her behind, so to speak. But she went right on talking about some fellow who was far out of it, or something like that.

It was most frustrating, you can imagine.

The elevator operator in my office building was asleep—well, not *quite*, but Wolfgang (that's his name, and he's not even German, isn't that annoying?) always *looked* as though he were sleeping—in his cage. I prodded him and capered about him and, as a final resort, cuffed him on the ear, but he continued to lie there against the wall, with his eyes shut, perched on his little pull-down seat. Finally, in annoyance, I took the elevator up myself, after booting him out onto the lobby tiles. By then I had realized, of course, that whatever strange malady had befallen me, I was to all intents and purposes invisible. It seemed impossible, even if I was invisible, that people should not notice their backsides being slapped or their bodies being kicked onto the tiles or their elevators stolen, but apparently such was the case.

I was so confused by then—but oddly enough, not in the slightest terrified—I was half belligerent and half pixilated with my own limitless abilities. Visions of movie stars and great wealth danced before my eyes.

And disappeared as rapidly.

What good were women or wealth if there was no one to share it with you? Even the women. So the thoughts of being the greatest bank robber in history passed from me, and I resigned myself to getting out—if "out" was the proper term—getting out of this predicament.

I left the elevator on the twenty-sixth floor and walked down the hall to the office door. It read the same as it had read for twenty-seven years:

RAMES & KLAUS
DIAMOND APPRAISERS
JEWELRY EXPERTS

I shoved open the door, and for a second my heart leaped in my throat that perhaps till now it had all been a colossal hoax. For Fritz Klaus—big, red-faced Fritz with the small mole beside his mouth—was screaming at me.

"Winsocki! You dolt! How many times have I told you when they go back in the pinch-bags, pull tight the cords! A hundred thousand dollars on the floor for the scrubwoman! Winsocki! You imbecile!"

But he was not screaming at me. He was scream-ing, that was all. But really, it was no surprise. Klaus and George Rames never actually talked to me . . . or even bothered to shout at me. They knew I did my job—had, in fact, been doing it for twenty-seven years—with method and attentiveness, and so they took me for granted. The shouting was all part of the office.

Klaus just had to scream. But he was directing his screams at the air, not at me. After all, how *could* he be screaming at me? I wasn't even there.

He went down on his knees and began picking up the little uncut rough diamonds he had spilled, and when he had them all, he went down further on his stomach, so his vest was dirtied by the floor, and looked under my bench.

When he was satisfied, he got up and brushed him-self off . . . and walked away. As far as he knew, I was working. Or in his view of the world, was I just eliminated? It was a puzzler, but no matter . . . I was not there. I was gone.

I turned around and went back down the hall.

The elevator was gone.

I had to wait a long time till I could get to the lobby.

No cars would stop for my ring.

I had to wait till someone else on that floor wanted down.

That was when the real horror of it all hit me.

How strange. . . .

I had been quiet all my life; I had married quietly and lived quietly, and now I had not even the one single pleasure of dying with a bang. Even that had been taken from me. I had just sort of snuffed out like a candle. How or why or when was no matter. I had been robbed of that one noise I thought was mine, inevitable as taxes. But even that had been deprived me. I was a shadow . . . a ghost in a real world. And for the first time in my life, all the bottled-up frustrations I had never known were banked inside me burst forth. I was shocked through and through and down with horror, but instead of crying, I hit someone.

I hit him as hard as I could. In the elevator there. I hit him full in the face, and I felt his nose skew over, as blood ran darkly on his face, and my knuckles hurt, and I hit him again, so my hand would slide in the blood, because I was Albert Winsocki and they had taken away my dying. They had made me quieter still. I had never bothered anyone, and I was hardly noticed, and when I would finally have had someone mourn for me and notice me and think about me as myself alone . . . I had been robbed!

I hit him a third time, and his nose broke.

He never noticed.

He left the elevator, covered with blood, and never even flinched.

Then I cried.

For a long time. The elevator kept going up and down with me in it, and no one heard my crying.

Finally, I got out and walked the streets till it was dark.

Two weeks can be a short time. If you are in love. If you are wealthy and seek adventure. If you have no cares and only pleasures. If you are healthy, and the world is fine and live and beckoning. Two weeks can be a short time.

Two weeks.

Those next two weeks were the longest in my life. Alone. Completely, agonizingly alone, in the midst of crowds. In the neoned heart of town I stood in the center of the street and shrieked at the passing throngs. I was nearly run down.

Two weeks of wandering, sleeping where I wanted to sleep—park benches, the honeymoon suite at the Waldorf, my own bed at home—and eating where I wanted to eat. I took what I wanted; it wasn't stealing, precisely; if I hadn't eaten, I would have starved—yet it was all emptiness.

I went home several times, but Alma was carrying on just nicely without me. Carrying on was the word. I would never have thought Alma could do it, particularly with the weight she had put on the past few years . . . but there he was.

George Rames. My boss. I corrected myself . . . my ex-boss.

So I felt no real duty to home and wife.

Alma had the house and she had Zasu. And, it appeared, she had George Rames. That fat oaf!

By the end of two weeks, I was a wreck. I was unshaved and dirty, but who cared? Who could see me . . . or would have cared had they been able to!

My original belligerence had turned into a more concrete antagonism toward everyone. Unsuspecting people in the streets were pummeled by me as I passed, should the inclination strike me. I kicked women and slapped children. . . . I was indifferent to the pain of those I struck. What was their pain compared to *my* pain—especially when none of them cried. It was all in my mind. I actually *craved* a scream or whine from one of them. For such an evidence of pain would have been a reminder that I was in their ken, that at least I existed.

But no such sound came.

Two weeks? Hell! Paradise Lost! It was a little over two weeks from the day Zasu had snubbed me, and I had more or less made my home in the lobby of the St. Moritz-on-the-Park. I was lying there on a couch, with a hat I had borrowed from a passerby over my eyes, when that animal urge to strike out overcame me. I swung my legs down and shoved the hat back on my head. I saw a man in a trench coat leaning against the cigar counter, reading a newspaper and chuckling to himself. That cruddy dog, I thought, what the hell is *he* laughing about?

It so infuriated me, I got up and lunged at him. He saw me coming and sidestepped. I, of course, expected him to go right on reading, even when I swung on him, and his movement took me by surprise. I went into the cigar case and it caught me in the stomach, knocking the wind from me.

"Ta-ta, buddy," the man in the trench coat chastised me, waggling a lean finger in my face. "Now that isn't polite at all, is it? To hit a man who can't even see you."

He took me by the collar and the seat of my pants and threw me across the lobby. I went flailing through a rack of picture postcards and landed on my stomach. I slid across the polished floor and brought up against the revolving door.

I didn't even feel the pain. I sat up, there on the floor, and looked at him. He stood there with his hands on his hips, laughing uproariously at me. I stared and my mouth dropped open. I was speechless.

"Catching flies, buddy?"

I was so amazed, I left my mouth open.

"Y-you, you can *see* me!" I was whooping. "You can *see* me!"

He gave a rueful little snort and turned away. "Of course I can." He started to walk away, then stopped and said, over his shoulder, "You don't think I'm one of *them,* do you?" and crooked his thumb at the people rushing about in the lobby.

It had never dawned on me.

I had thought I was alone in this thing.

But here was another like me!

Not for a second did I consider the possibility that he could see me, while the others could not, and still be a part of their world. It was apparent from the moment he threw me across the lobby that he was in the same predicament I was. But somehow he seemed more at ease about it all. As though this were one great party, and he the host.

He started to walk away.

I scrambled to my feet as he was pressing the button for the elevator, wondering why he was doing that. The elevator couldn't stop for him if it was human-operated, as I'd seen it was.

"Uh, hey! Wait a minute, there—"

The elevator came down, and an old man in baggy pants was running it. "I was on six, Mr. Jim. Heard it and came right down."

The old man smiled at the man in the trench coat—Jim it was—and Jim clapped him on the shoulder. "Thanks, Denny. I'd like to go up to my room."

I started after them, but Jim gave Denny a nudge, and inclined his head in my direction with a disgusted expression on his face. "Up, Denny," he said.

The elevator doors started to close. I ran up.

"Hey! Wait a second. My name is Winsocki. Albert Winsocki, like in the song, *you* known, 'Buckle down, Win—' "

The doors closed almost on my nose.

I was frantic. The only other person (*persons,* I realized with a start) who could see me, and they were going away. . . . I might search and never find them.

I was *so* frantic, in fact, I almost missed the easiest way to trace them. I looked up and the floor indicator arrow was going up, up, up to stop at the tenth floor. I waited till another elevator came down, with the ones who could not see me in it, and tossed out the operator . . . and took it up myself.

I had to search all through the corridors of the tenth floor till I heard his voice through a door, talking to the old man.

He was saying, "One of the newer ones, Denny. A boor, a completely obnoxious lower form of life."

And Denny replied, "Chee, Mr. Jim, I just like to sit an' hear ya talk. Wit' all them college words. I was real unhappy till you come along, ya know?"

"Yes, Denny, I know." It was a condescending tone of voice if ever I'd heard one.

I knew he'd never open the door, so I went looking for the maid from that floor. She had her ring of keys in her apron and never even noticed me taking them. I started back for the room, and stopped.

I thought a moment and ran back to the elevator. I went downstairs and climbed into the booth where the bills were paid, where all the cash was stored. I found what I was after in one of the till drawers. I shoved it into my coat pocket and went back upstairs.

At the door I hesitated. Yes, I could still hear them babbling. I used the skeleton key to get inside.

When I threw open the door, the man named Jim leaped from the bed and glared at me. "What are you doing in here? Get out at once, or I shall *throw* you out!"

He started toward me.

I pulled what I had gotten from the till drawer from my pocket and pointed it at him. "Now just settle back, Mr. Jim, and there won't be any trouble."

He raised his hands very melodramatically and started backward till his knee-backs caught the edge of the bed, and he sat down with a plop.

"Oh, take down your hands," I said. "You look like a bad Western movie." His hands came down self-consciously.

Denny looked at me. "What's he doin', Mr. Jim?"

"I don't know, Denny; I don't know," Jim said slowly, with thought. His eyes were trained on the barrel of the short-nosed revolver I held. His eyes were frightened.

I found myself shaking. I tried to hold the revolver steady, but it wavered in my hand. "I'm nervous, fellow," I said, partly to let him note it, as if he hadn't already, and half to reassure myself that I was master of the situation. "Don't make me any worse than I am right now."

He sat very still, his lowered hands folded in his lap.

"For two weeks now, I've been close to going insane. My wife couldn't see or hear or feel me. No one in the street could. No one for two weeks. It's like I'm dead . . . and today I found you two. You're the only ones like me! Now I want to know what this is all about. What's happened to me?"

Denny looked at Mr. Jim, and then at me.

"Hey, is he cuckoo, Mr. Jim? You want I should slug him, Mr. Jim?"

The old man could never have made it.

Jim saw that much, to his credit.

"No, Denny. Sit where you are. The man wants some information. I think it's only fair I give it to him." He looked at me. His face was soft, like a sponge.

"My name is Thompson, Mr.—ah—Mr. . . . What did you say your name was?"

"Winsocki. Albert Winsocki. Like in the song."

"Oh yes, Mr. Winsocki. Well." His poise and sneering manner were returning as he saw he had at least had the edge on me in information. "The reason for your current state of non-noticeability—you aren't really insubstantial, you know . . . that gun could kill me . . . a truck could run us down and we'd be dead—the reason is very complex. I'm afraid I can't give you any scientific explanations, and I'm not even sure there are any. Let's put it this way. . . ."

He crossed his legs, and I steadied the gun on him. He went on. "There are forces in the world today, Mr. Winsocki, that are invisibly working to make us all carbon copies of one another. Forces that force us into molds of each other. You walk down the street and you never see anyone's face, really. You sit faceless in a movie or hidden from sight in a dreary living room watching television. When you pay bills or car fares or talk to people, they see the job they're doing—but never you.

"With some of us, this is carried even further. We are so unnoticeable about it—wallflowers, you might say—all through our lives, that when these forces that crush us into one mold work enough to get us where they want us, we just—poof!—disappear to all those around us. Do you understand?"

I stared at him.

I knew what he was talking about, of course. Who could fail to notice it in this great machine world we'd made for ourselves? So that was it. I had been made like everyone else, but had been so negative a personality before, it had completely blanked me out to everyone. It was like a filter on a camera. Put a red filter on and everything red was there—but not there. That was the way with me. The cameras in everyone had been filtered against me. And Mr. Jim and Denny and—

"Are there more like us?"

Mr. Jim spread his hands. "Why, there are dozens, Winsocki. Dozens. Soon there will be hundreds, and then thousands. With things going the way they are . . . with people buying in supermarkets and eating in drive-ins and TV advertising . . . why, I'd say we could be expecting more company all the time.

"But not me."

I looked at him, and then at Denny. Denny was blank, so I looked back at Thompson. "What do you mean?"

"Mr. Winsocki," he explained patiently but condescendingly, "I was a college professor. Nothing really brilliant, mind you, in fact I suppose I was dullness personified to my students. But I know my subject. Phoenician Art, it was. But my students came in and went out and never saw me. The faculty never had cause to reprimand me, and so after a while I started to fade out. Then I was gone, like you.

"I wandered around, as you must still be doing,

but soon I realized what a fine life it was. No responsibility, no taxes, no struggling for existence. Just live the way I wish, and take what I want. I even have Denny here—he was a handyman no one paid attention to—as my friend and manservant. I like this life, Mr. Winsocki. That was why I was not too anxious to make your acquaintance. I dislike seeing the *status quo* upset."

I realized I was listening to a madman.

Mr. Jim Thompson had been a poor teacher and had suffered my fate. But where I had been turned—as I now realized—from a milquetoasted humdrummer to a man cunning enough to find a revolver, and adventurous enough to use it, he had been turned into a monomaniac.

This was his kingdom.

But there were others.

Finally, I saw there was no point talking to him. The forces that had crushed us till we were so small the rest of the world could not see us had done their work all too well on him. He was lost. He was satisfied with being unseen, unheard, unknown.

So was Denny. They were complacent. More than that . . . they were overjoyed. And during this past year I have found many like them. All the same. But I am not like that. I want out of here. I want you to see me again.

I'm trying desperately, the only way I know how.

It may sound stupid, but when people are daydreaming or unfocused on life, so to speak, they may catch sight of me. I'm working on that. I keep whistling and humming. Have you ever heard me? The song is "Buckle Down, Winsocki."

Have you ever caught sight of me, just out of the

corner of your eye, and thought it was a trick of your imagination?

Have you ever thought you heard a radio or TV playing that song, and there was no radio or TV?

Please! I'm begging you! Listen for me. I'm right here, and I'm humming in your ear so you'll hear me and help me.

"Buckle Down, Winsocki," that's the tune. Can you hear it?

Are you listening?

The Lottery in Babylon

BY JORGE LUIS BORGES

translated by John M. Fein

Jorge Luis Borges, the great fantasist from Argentina, is finally becoming as well known in the United States as he is in South America. His stories are richly imagined, thoughtful views of realities that might be or might have been—as in this short tale of the strange way in which chance was introduced into the affairs of the world.

*L*ike all men in Babylon, I have been proconsul; like all, a slave. I have also known omnipotence, opprobrium, imprisonment. Look: the index finger on my right hand is missing. Look: through the rip in my cape you can see a vermilion tattoo on my stomach. It is the second symbol, Beth. This letter, on nights when the moon is full, gives me power over men whose mark is Gimmel, but it subordinates me to the men of Aleph, who on moonless nights owe obedience to those marked with Gimmel. In the half-light of dawn, in a cellar, I have cut the jugular vein of sacred bulls before a black stone. During a lunar year I have been declared invisible. I shouted and they did not answer me; I stole bread and they did not behead me. I have known what the Greeks do not know, incertitude. In a bronze chamber, before the silent handkerchief of the strangler, hope has been faithful to me, as has panic in the river of pleasure. Heraclides Ponticus tells with amazement that Pythagoras remembered having been Pyrrhus and before that Euphorbus and before that some other mortal. In order to remember similar vicissitudes I do not need to have recourse to death or even to deception.

I owe this almost atrocious variety to an institution which other republics do not know or which operates in them in an imperfect and secret manner: the lottery. I have not looked into its history; I know that the wise men cannot agree. I know of its powerful purposes what a man who is not versed in astrology can know about the moon. I come from a dizzy land where the lottery is the basis of reality. Until today I have thought as little about it as I have about the conduct of indecipherable divinities or about my heart. Now, far from Babylon and its beloved customs, I think with a certain amount of amazement about the lottery and about the blasphemous conjectures which veiled men murmur in the twilight.

My father used to say that formerly—a matter of centuries, of years?—the lottery in Babylon was a game of plebeian character. He recounted (I don't know whether rightly) that barbers sold, in exchange for copper coins, squares of bone or of parchment adorned with symbols. In broad daylight a drawing took place. Those who won received silver coins without any other test of luck. The system was elementary, as you can see.

Naturally these "lotteries" failed. Their moral virtue was nil. They were not directed at all of man's faculties, but only at hope. In the face of public indifference, the merchants who founded these venal lotteries began to lose money. Someone tried a reform: The interpolation of a few unfavorable tickets in the list of favorable numbers. By means of this reform, the buyers of numbered squares ran the double risk of winning a sum and of paying a fine that could be considerable. This slight danger (for every thirty favorable numbers there was one unlucky one) awoke, as is natural, the interest of the public. The Babylonians threw themselves into the game. Those who did not acquire chances were considered pusillanimous, cowardly. In time, that justified disdain was doubled. Those who did not play were scorned, but also the losers who paid the fine were scorned. The Company (as it came to be known then) had to take care of the winners, who could not cash in their prizes if almost the total amount of the fines was unpaid. It started a lawsuit against the losers. The judge condemned them to pay the original fine and costs or spend several days in jail. All chose jail in order to defraud the Company. The bravado of a few is the source of the omnipotence of the Company and of its metaphysical and ecclesiastical power.

A little while afterward the lottery lists omitted the amounts of fines and limited themselves to publishing the days of imprisonment that each unfavorable number indicated. That laconic spirit, almost unnoticed at the time, was of capital importance. *It was the first appearance in the lottery of nonmonetary elements.* The success was tremendous. Urged by the clientele, the Company was obliged to increase the unfavorable numbers.

Everyone knows that the people of Babylon are fond of logic and even of symmetry. It was illogical for the lucky numbers to be computed in round coins and the unlucky ones in days and nights of imprisonment. Some moralists reasoned that the possession of money does not always determine happiness and that other forms of happiness are perhaps more direct.

Another concern swept the quarters of the poorer classes. The members of the college of priests multiplied their stakes and enjoyed all the vicissitudes of terror and hope; the poor (with reasonable or unavoidable envy) knew that they were excluded from that notoriously delicious rhythm. The just desire that all, rich and poor, should participate equally in the lottery inspired an indignant agitation, the memory of which the years have not erased. Some obstinate people did not understand (or pretended not to understand) that it was a question of a new order, of a necessary historical stage. A slave stole a crimson ticket, which in the drawing credited him with the burning of his tongue. The legal code fixed that same penalty for the one who stole a ticket. Some Babylonians argued that he deserved the burning irons in his status of a thief; others, generously, that the executioner should apply it to him because chance had determined it that way. There were disturbances; there were lamentable drawings of blood; but the masses of Babylon finally imposed their will against the opposition of the rich. The people achieved amply its generous purposes. In the first place, it caused the Company to accept total power. (That unification was necessary, given the vastness and complexity of the new operations.) In the second place, it made the lottery secret, free, and general. The mercenary sale of chances was abolished. Once initiated in the mysteries of Baal, every free man automatically participated in the sacred drawings, which took place in the labyrinths of the god every sixty nights and which determined his destiny until the next drawing. The consequences were incalculable. A fortunate play could bring about his promotion to the council of wise men or the imprisonment of an enemy (public or private) or finding, in the peaceful darkness of his room, the woman who begins to excite him and whom he never expected to see again. A bad play: mutilation, different kinds of infamy, death. At times one single fact—the vulgar murder of C, the mysterious apotheosis of B—was the happy solution of thirty or forty drawings. To combine the plays was difficult, but one must remember that the individuals of the Company were (and are) omnipotent and astute. In many cases the knowledge that certain happinesses were the simple product of chance would have diminished their virtue. To avoid that obstacle, the agents of the Company made use of the power of suggestion and magic. Their steps, their maneuverings were secret. To find out about the intimate hopes and terrors of each individual, they had astrologists and spies. There were certain stone lions; there was a sacred latrine called Qaphwa; there were fissures in a dusty aqueduct which, according to general opinion, *led to the Company;* malignant or benevolent persons deposited information in these places. An alphabetical file collected these items of varying truthfulness.

Incredibly, there were complaints. The Company, with its usual discretion, did not answer directly. It preferred to scrawl in the rubbish of a mask factory a brief statement which now figures in the sacred scriptures. This doctrinal item observed that the lottery is an interpolation of chance in the order of the world and that to accept errors is not to contradict chance: it is to corroborate it. It likewise observed that those lions and that sacred receptacle, although not disavowed by the Company (which did not abandon the right to consult them), functioned without official guarantee.

This declaration pacified the public's restlessness. It also produced other effects, perhaps unforeseen by its writer. It deeply modified the spirit and the operations of the Company. I don't have much time left; they tell us that the ship is about to weigh anchor. But I shall try to explain it.

However unlikely it might seem, no one had tried out before then a general theory of chance. Babylonians are not very speculative. They revere the judgments of fate; they deliver to them their lives, their hopes, their panic; but it does not occur to them to investigate fate's labyrinthine laws nor the gyratory spheres which reveal it. Nevertheless, the *unofficial* declaration that I have mentioned inspired many discussions of judicial-mathematical character. From some one of them the following conjecture was born: If the lottery is an intensification of chance, a periodic infusion of chaos in the cosmos, would it not be right for chance to intervene in all stages of the drawing and not in one alone? Is it not ridiculous for chance to dictate someone's death and have the circumstances of that death—secrecy, publicity, the fixed time of an hour or a century—not subject to chance? These just scruples finally caused a considerable reform, whose complexities (aggravated by centuries' practice) only a few specialists understand, but which I shall try to summarize, at least in a symbolic way.

Let us imagine a first drawing, which decrees the death of a man. For its fulfillment one proceeds to another drawing, which proposes (let us say) nine possible executors. Of these executors, four can initiate a third drawing which will tell the name of the executioner; two can replace the adverse order with a fortunate one (finding a treasure, let us say); another will intensify the death penalty (that is, will make it infamous or enrich it with tortures); others can refuse to fulfill it. This is the symbolic scheme. In reality *the number of drawings is infinite.* No decision is final, all branch into others. Ignorant people suppose that infinite drawings require an infinite time; actually it is sufficient for time to be infinitely subdivisible, as the famous parable of the contest with the tortoise teaches. This infinity harmonizes admirably with the sinuous numbers of Chance and with the Celestial Archetype of the Lottery, which the Platonists adore. Some warped echo of our rites seems to have resounded on the Tiber; Ellus Lampridius, in the *Life of Antoninus Heliogabalus,* tells that this emperor wrote on shells the lots that were destined for his guests, so that one received ten pounds of gold and another ten flies, ten dormice, ten bears. It is permissible to recall that Heliogabalus was brought up in Asia Minor, among the priests of the eponymous god.

There are also impersonal drawings, with an indefinite purpose. One decrees that a sapphire of Taprobana be thrown into the waters of the Euphrates;

another, that a bird be released from the roof of a tower; another, that each century there be withdrawn (or added) a grain of sand from the innumerable ones on the beach. The consequences are, at times, terrible.

Under the beneficent influence of the Company, our customs are saturated with chance. The buyer of a dozen amphoras of Damascene wine will not be surprised if one of them contains a talisman or a snake. The scribe who writes a contract almost never fails to introduce some erroneous information. I myself, in this hasty declaration, have falsified some splendor, some atrocity. Perhaps, also, some mysterious monotony. . . . Our historians, who are the most penetrating on the globe, have invented a method to correct chance. It is well known that the operations of this method are (in general) reliable, although, naturally, they are not divulged without some portion of deceit. Furthermore, there is nothing so contaminated with fiction as the history of the Company. A paleographic document, exhumed in a temple, can be the result of yesterday's lottery or of an age-old lottery. No book is published without some discrepancy in each one of the copies. Scribes take a secret oath to omit, to interpolate, to change. The indirect lie is also cultivated.

The Company, with divine modesty, avoids all publicity. Its agents, as is natural, are secret. The orders which it issues continually (perhaps incessantly) do not differ from those lavished by imposters. Moreover, who can brag about being a mere impostor? The drunkard who improvises an absurd order, the dreamer who awakens suddenly and strangles the woman who sleeps at his side, do they not execute perhaps, a secret decision of the Company? That silent functioning, comparable to God's, gives rise to all sorts of conjectures. One abominably insinuates that the Company has not existed for centuries and that the sacred disorder of our lives is purely hereditary, traditional. Another judges it eternal and teaches that it will last until the last night, when the last god annihilates the world. Another declares that the Company is omnipotent, but that it only has influence in tiny things: in a bird's call, in the shadings of rust and of dust, in the half-dreams of dawn. Another, in the words of masked heresiarchs, *that it has never existed and will not exist.* Another, no less vile, reasons that it is indifferent to affirm or deny the reality of the shadowy corporation, because Babylon is nothing else than an infinite game of chance.

Dogman of Islington

BY HILARY BAILEY

Here's an amusing story about a bourgeois En-
glish family that discovers its dog can talk.
Being proper people, naturally they wouldn't
want to do the crude thing and exploit the dog
as a show-business freak—but extraordinary
situations create extraordinary problems. Hilary
Bailey's story is witty in its satire of the British
middle class . . . and rather sad, too.

There are two and a half million registered
dog addicts in Great Britain, and this figure does not
take into account those owners who live in sin with
their animals without benefit of Post Office.

The Galloways, a smart, middle-aged couple living
in an airy, comfortable home in North London—in
Islington, to be precise—acquired a nice, romping
puppy, a cross between a poodle and a terrier, with
several other breeds more or less represented. Sandy
was a medium-sized dog with a blunt muzzle, pricked
ears, curly black fur, a long spiky tail, and feathery
black feet.

The Galloway family consisted of Neil Galloway,
the editor of the Islington *Post,* the local paper of the
area in which they lived. Mr. Galloway had been
editor of the *Daily Record* before his collapse and

rehabilitation. His wife was Irena Galloway, the granddaughter of Count Ivan Bresnin. She worked in the Russian section of the BBC's External Services. Sophia Galloway, their eighteen-year-old daughter, worked as a photographic model, and Ivan, their twenty-year-old son, was studying physics at London University. Peripherally, there was Belinda Hodges, Mr. Galloway's secretary and right-hand woman on the *Post*—she and Irena were secretary and chairman, respectively, of the Islington branch of the Campaign for Peace—Piotr Razin, a victim of totalitarian communism, a Sovietologist and a distant relative of Irena's, Samuel, Michael, and James, Sophia's boy friends, and Samantha Jamieson, Ivan's girl friend.

The Galloways and their various friends were reasonably controlled and steady in a crisis—Irena, being Russian-born, was allowed a little latitude. They conducted their personal relationships in a civilized manner. They kept their passions for liberal politics. Whether they had feelings for those around them and elected not to display them, whether they had no feelings and had never had them, or whether they had once had them and they had shriveled up for want of practice was uncertain. But the fact remained that when the clinic telephoned Irena to inform her that her mother, the old countess, had died, Irena merely remarked, "Well, she was eighty-four." Neil said, "She had a good run for her money, at any rate." Sophia asked, "When's the funeral?" And Ivan asked, "Who's going over to sort everything out?" Each Galloway in his or her heart of hearts admired the others for their exercise of decent self-control and appreciated his or her own display of same.

Small wonder that this well-adapted and stable unit needed in their midst a warm, simple creature whose idiosyncrasies, instinctive responses, and richly human characteristics they could observe and comment on to each other during the lacunae of family life.

So when Sandy I had to be put down and Sandy II was offered to them by a neighbor whose poodle had been molested by an itinerant terrier, the Galloways accepted him gladly. Sandy's temerity, his gambolings, fanatic attachment to a pram rug which he constantly trailed over the parquet in his mouth, his peccadilloes in the curtain-tearing and floor-wetting line, all provided a source of innocent mirth and stimulating mild annoyance to counter the sound sense, enlightened views, and somewhat dismissive conversation of the Galloway family circle.

One breakfast, the strange event occurred. Seven-thirty, and Irena Galloway, cool and fresh in a subtly striped cotton dress, discreetly made up with a shilling's worth of kindly, odoriferous cosmetics, was scrambling eggs in her special way. Neil Galloway, in crisp business suit, read the *Times* calmly. Sophia, in a white ruffled peignoir, was examining her right eye—a shining cerulean orb fringed with jetty lashes —in a tiny magnifying mirror. Ivan, in well-pressed student attire, read the *Guardian*. Through the open back door, the garden, all green smooth lawn and colorful herbaceous borders, was revealed.

Their contemporaries often asked Sophia and Ivan why they did not move away from home. "But I love them," Sophia would reply out of her ripe, childish lips. "It's Mother's borscht," Ivan would say, glinting his slanted Nureyev-like eyes at his hearer. In actual fact, what with the children's car, the crisp ironing, the old family doctor, and the comfortable beds, Ivan and Sophia knew which side their bread was buttered on. No escape required for them from the stuffy living room, the fat cat, the snoozing granddad, and the smell of Yorkshire pudding. In the Galloway home all was modern, hygienic, and lavish.

The group was just putting fork to egg when Sandy burst in through the garden door and stood panting in the kitchen.

"Good morning, Sandy," Neil Galloway observed genially.

"Snuffle, snuffle," said Sophia in Sandy's direction.

"Here is your breakfast, doggy," Irena said agreeably in Russian.

Sandy trotted over to his plate.

"Nice," he said quite clearly in a rasping voice.

"What's that?"

"The dog spoke," said Irena and Neil Galloway together.

"Good heavens!"

"Surprise," said Sophia and Ivan together.

"What did you say, Sandy?" Irena said gently. But Sandy continued to snuffle and crunch down his breakfast.

"Well, well," said Neil Galloway. "That was quite extraordinary."

"I suppose with modified larynxes all dogs could speak," said Ivan.

"God forbid," said Irena.

"It might also be a question of the capacity to imitate," said Neil Galloway. "Young children, after all, learn to speak quite painfully. They're incomprehensible; they can't actually reproduce the sound they hear. But the imitative instinct is so strong that they persist."

"Hurry up, Neil, or you'll be late," said Irena.

The family ate up and then scattered to do the various things dictated to them by necessity and inner need. The kitchen, bright and clean, was empty but for Sandy, who was waiting.

There was a click as the front door opened and footsteps sounded on the checkered marble of the hall floor. Sandy's ears pricked up; he wagged his tail. The kitchen door opened and in came the sturdy, shiny-faced *au pair*, Valentina. The Galloways agreed that people who worked for you made complications and upset the balance of the family structure if they lived in, so Valentina lived with a Russian family round the corner and came in when the family had gone out. After the death of Sandy I, Irena, full of the rich humanity of the Old Russian landowner, as she wryly hinted, suggested that Valentina should come and occupy the spare room. Valentina refused, and the family, with some relief, got Sandy II.

Sandy began to jump about when he saw Valentina.

"Kood moornink, Sandy," said Valentina.

"Kood moornink, Walentina," said Sandy in his gruff voice, sounding like a boyar plotting against Ivan the Terrible in an archway.

Valentina began to collect the breakfast things from the table.

"I think," said Valentina carefully, "that I will put on the radio." She reached up and turned on the radio, switching to Radio One.

"There," said Valentina. "The radio is on and music is playing. Now I will wash the dishes."

Sandy wagged his tail. He enjoyed Valentina, who

was always doing something interesting and gave him sweet biscuits to eat. They helped each other with their English.

Valentina washed the dishes. "Now," she said encouragingly to herself, "I will collect the dirty laundry from the laundry basket, which is in the bathroom."

Sandy was first out of the door, up the stairs, and into the bathroom.

So Valentina collected the laundry, went into the kitchen, put various items in the sink to soak, placed the others on the drain board, holding up, with a smile of mingled admiration and contempt, Sophia's ruffled petticoat and then replacing it. As she worked, Valentina named the items she was handling and described her actions to herself in the careful manner of a Linguaphone record. Sandy hung round her feet, pattering backward as she moved, wagging his tail, lolling his tongue and occasionally growling a word to himself under his breath.

Valentina then tucked her skirt into her drawers, took a bucket from under the sink, took a somewhat worn-down scrubbing brush and a cloth, went into the hall and began to scrub the tiles.

Sandy stood in the kitchen doorway watching as she scrubbed the immaculate squares. Light fell into the hall and onto the stooped figure of Valentina. She put away the bucket and watered the two trees and the plants which adorned the hall.

"Now," she said. "It is time for morning coffee." Sandy jumped up and down and skidded quickly into the kitchen, his oversized black feet sliding on the blue-patterned vinyl of the kitchen floor.

Valentina made the coffee from a packet she had

brought with her and put it in her special mug. She sat down on one chair and put her feet on another. Sandy sat beside her, flopping his tail up and down on the blue vinyl. His eyes were fastened on Valentina's face.

Valentina eventually looked down at him. "Yes, Sandy," she prompted him.

Sandy's tail hit the floor in giant thumps. "Biscuit," he rasped.

"Say please, please," said Valentina.

"Please," said Sandy in his heavily accented English.

Valentina had in fact cautioned Sandy long and hard against exercising his talent in front of the family. She could not have explained why she did this but, impressed by her sincerity, Sandy developed a strong conditioning against using words in front of the Galloways.

Months passed. And Sandy's small vocabulary expanded. Neil Galloway edited the Islington *Post* and worked late some nights. Irena worked at the BBC and on the Campaign for Peace with Belinda and attended cultural events at the Anglo-Soviet club with her relative, Piotr Razin. Sophia was photographed and went to parties, dances, and balls with Samuel, Michael, and James. Ivan worked hard at the University and went about with Samantha Jamieson.

The Galloways' regular monthly dinner parties also took place. On one such evening the guests were Belinda, Neil Galloway's right-hand woman, Irena's relative, Piotr Razin, two of Sophia's friends, Michael and James, Samantha Jamieson, Ivan's girl friend, Nigel Hogarth, poet and publisher, and old Doctor Nugent.

Irena's dinners were known throughout the length and breadth of Islington and greatly looked forward to by all those invited to them. Five courses, ground, pulverized, and sieved—if Irena could have made salt by grinding two other ingredients together, she would have done so—and the guests were ecstatic. With each course—borscht, Albanian cured fish, *tête de veau*, an Indian pudding and Greek cheese, followed by those little Serbian savories for which Irena was so famous—Irena described the trek to Canonbury, Bethnal Green, and Harrow for rare and exotic ingredients. The guests fell about with mingled appreciation and guilt at merely devouring the fruits of such labor. Meanwhile the conversation ranged intelligently over the atrocities of the war in Vietnam, the color bar in England, and a nasty rape case reported in the park nearby. Valentina carried things in and out and was jested with gaily in Russian by Piotr Razin. She replied with the bright smile of one reared in a small village where it does not pay to offend anybody.

Fainting with food, liberal principles, wine, and the raptures they had gone into over their food, the guests rolled into the living room. The French doors at the end of the room were opened onto the garden. The floor, the grand piano, the table shone like mirrors.

"Piotr will sing," announced Irena simply.

She played the piano while Piotr sang Russian songs both grave and gay.

After the recital, man's inhumanity to man and other topics were again discussed.

"I felt," said Nigel Hogarth, "that Melanie's unconscious intention was to attack my ego at its weakest point."

"It's extraordinary," said Doctor Nugent, "how few women understand their own bodies."

"The roots of aggression," said Neil Galloway, "are with the primitive."

"But," said Irena, "xenophobia is a condition of man, as I know too well."

"Oh," said Sophia, "if only we could love one another more."

"Discoveries in the biological sciences," said Ivan, "will soon alter all that."

Sandy, having gleaned the palatable scraps from Valentina, left her sturdily washing up in the kitchen and came into the room wagging his tail.

"Delightful dog," said Doctor Nugent, trying to pat him. Sandy went and lay down in the corner to watch everything.

The light fell softly on the group: Neil, drink in hand, standing by the piano, Irena gesturing gently as she spoke, Doctor Nugent planted in his chair looking so reliable, the entrancing Sophia on the sofa with Michael and James on either side, Ivan and Samantha, hand in hand, sitting on the floor, and the vital Nigel Hogarth sprawled challengingly in his chair.

Sandy glanced from face to face.

Then Irena said, "After all, a woman's first job is the family. The mechanical jobs, cooking, washing, clearing up, are not intrinsically very valuable, but the whole—"

And Sandy, from the corner, said in a strong Russian accent, "Valentina washes my floor." Then he lolled sideways on the parquet, flopping his tail heavily, lolling his tongue and staring round at everyone.

There was a pause while all present worked out their reactions.

"Oh, God, so it was true," groaned Irena.

"Sort of stomach-turning," declared Sophia.

The older Galloway stared at Sandy carefully. The guests looked interested.

"Does your dog speak, then?" Nigel Hogarth asked neutrally.

Doctor Nugent's eyes glinted. "You ought to offer him for some kind of research," he said.

"Get him on television and make a fortune," said Michael, Sophia's boy friend.

Neil Galloway cleared his throat. "Sandy is a domestic pet," he stated. "I do not intend to offer him for scientific research or public display. He is a dog."

"An animal should be treated as an animal," said Irena.

Sandy glanced about him, the motion of his tail stopping gradually like an arrested metronome. Far from gaining any praise or kindness or, better still, the biscuit Valentina normally offered him at his better strokes, he saw only disapproving faces. He got up and slunk from the room. The guests watched him go.

"It seems a pity," Doctor Nugent remarked carefully, "to ignore the phenomenon completely."

He was interrupted by Nigel Hogarth's coarse roar of laughter. Hogarth threw himself back in his half-egg-shaped basket chair, nearly overturning himself, poked out his spindly legs, and laughed in vulgar gusts.

"Arharharhar," he roared. "I wouldn't fancy having him about—arharharhar—he might come out with some ripe takes about you—arhar."

Neil Galloway stood up. Irena, meeting the manifest coarseness of the petty bourgeois, took on a frozen expression.

"I say, though," remarked Belinda clearly, "he would look splendid on television."

"That's really a bit sordid, Belinda," said Ivan. "You'll suggest selling him to a circus next."

"Ugh." Sophia shuddered her narrow shoulders. "Those poor creatures. Shut up, Belinda."

Nigel Hogarth's snorts subsided. He pulled himself to his feet and walked toward Irena with his hands extended. "I'm terribly sorry, Irena," I said. "I really must have had too much wine. I'd better depart."

Irena smiled a cool smile and preceded him out of the room and down the hall. And so Hogarth made his way down the trim path and out into the night, like Napoleon after Waterloo, knowing that the expensive and tasteful facilities of the Galloway home were now barred to him forever. He headed toward the Duck and Dragon to tell his story, which would not, of course, be believed.

"I'd really prefer it," Neil Galloway said, glancing masterfully round his circle and pouring himself another drink, "if no one mentioned this Sandy episode out of doors. Sandy is a dog. If the news gets out, we'll have the TV, newspapers, everyone round our necks, pestering us and the dog. It would be most undesirable."

"Poor old woolly dog," said Sophia. "Let's call him in and give him a pat."

They called Sandy, who was crouching in the corner of the kitchen. He heard their voices, but would not come. Valentina, who had just left, had pried from him the story of his lapse and smacked him hard. The whole incident had set up a series of unfortunate associations in Sandy. "You will get yourself into serious trouble, Sandy," Valentina had warned him, but something had told her that already Sandy's doggy game was up.

Eventually Sandy went into the living room. He ran about snuffling and wuffling, receiving pats and affectionate comment. Irena even gave him a piece of chocolate. The balance of nature was restored.

After this painful incident, Sandy behaved himself, barking, snuffling, sliding over the blue vinyl on his giant feathery feet. He even behaved himself so far as to misbehave behind the living room curtains. Sometimes, from the depths of his basket would come a low mutter as Sandy reminded himself of his vocabulary. But these mutters were very indistinct and completely ignored by the Galloways. Sandy was a real favorite, quite one of the family.

Nevertheless, that tattered fragment of childhood innocence no longer spread automatically over the faces of the Galloways as their eyes lit on Sandy. They began, without realizing it, to shut doors against him. This made the dog unhappy.

One evening the family assembled after dinner when the doorbell rang.

"Belinda!" Irena said delightedly.

"Irena!" said Belinda. And the two women kissed.

Neil Galloway, on his fourth drink, looked for some reason displeased. "What brings you here, Belinda?" he asked petulantly.

"Business," Belinda replied shortly.

"Well, you know where the coffee pot is," said Irena. "I think I'll go now and leave you to it."

"That's right," said Belinda in a curious tone, as if this action of Irena's was no more than she expected.

Sophia and Ivan, who had been playing chess, smelled trouble and decided to evaporate also.

Neil Galloway and Belinda conducted the first part of their business on the sofa, unaware of the rolling, neutral eyes of Sandy sitting outside the French windows with his head on one side.

This over, Belinda went into the kitchen without a word and made coffee. Neil Galloway sprawled in an armchair, slightly muzzy.

When Belinda came back he said, "Well, what's the news, if any?"

"I'll tell you the news," said Belinda. "A letter arrived after you left today. The firm's accountant is coming on Wednesday."

Neil Galloway passed a hand over his clammy brow.

Now, it might have been wondered how, on their two salaries, the Galloways maintained their unostentatious but nevertheless very ample way of life— Valentina, the children's car, Neil's car, which was large, the food, the drinks, the friends, the laundry, and the children themselves, neither of whom could have been called a financial asset. People naturally assumed that Irena's mother, the countess, had not left Russia without the family jewels strapped round her then tiny waist. This was not true. The truth was that, faced with a drop in salary after getting the sack from the *Daily Record,* Neil Galloway had taken to speculation. For historic reasons, the editor of the Islington *Post* also had some of the functions of a business manager. Neil's system was this: Each month checks came in direct from retailers to his desk. And each month he abstracted two of the checks from the six biggest retailers. The sum he obtained was something like a hundred pounds a month. This, and his large overdraft, was tiding the family over fairly nicely. The children took their standard of living for granted. Irena shrewdly asked herself no questions about the fount of cash from which Neil drew. It was, of course, only a matter of time before Neil began to draw even more largely on the Islington *Post* funds. But time was running out.

Once again he passed a cold hand over his brow. "Don't worry, darling," he said. "I'll think of something."

"I hope so, darling," Belinda said neutrally.

She left, after kissing him tepidly in the hall. Neil stared after her as she tripped down the path in the fifteen-guinea boots he had bought her, giving no backward glance. He walked slowly back into the living room, sat down, and poured himself another drink. He had the weekend and two clear working days until the accountant started work. He had four days in which to replace the money, something like eight hundred pounds, he had taken since he began the job. The bank's regard for him was cool; they would never lend him another eight hundred. Irena, if she had it—as she well might—would never lend it to him. If he asked her to sell something, she would refuse, making a quiet fuss. Belinda, he realized, if she had anything, would never let go of it for him. Neil finished his drink and buried his head in his hands. He was desolate, first in the face of ruin and second in the face of those who would not help him. "Only Sophia," he moaned secretly, "would help me." And she would have, it is true, with a curl of the lip which said father is a baby.

Neil went to bed. Between the emerald sheets he

gazed at the broad, strong back of Irena, sleeping her usual sound sleep. Alone in the darkness, tears of remorse and loneliness coursed down his cheeks.

In the middle of the night he awoke foul-mouthed and exulting. He had the idea that would save them— sell Sandy! My God, why hadn't he thought of it before? Any one of a dozen firms would want him— circuses, films, anything. The dog was worth a fortune, and he had not even thought of it. All that anxiety for nothing and the eight hundred pounds was in front of his nose all the time.

Neil, restored absolutely, jumped out of bed and went down to the kitchen. As he opened the door Sandy sprang up, started to wag his tail, then backed away slightly.

"Sandy, old man," Neil began. Sandy looked at him. Neil put the kettle on to boil and, rather self-consciously, gave Sandy some dog biscuits.

"It seems to me," Neil said, standing embarrassedly in the middle of the floor in his pajamas talking to the dog, "that we should have a talk."

A cowed look came into Sandy's eyes. He dropped his head.

"How are you, Sandy?" said Neil anxiously.

Sandy, too well conditioned by Valentina, wagged his tail and looked expectantly at Neil.

"Really talk, I mean," Neil said.

There was a silence. Sandy stood in the corner of the kitchen watching Neil out of the corner of his eye. Neil made himself some coffee, sat down at the kitchen table, drank it, and smoked a cigarette, considering the crisis of Sandy collapsed in a corner, and shut his eyes.

If he doesn't speak up, I'm ruined, reasoned Neil. But he will bloody well speak up, and that's that.

"Sandy," he said. "If you'll talk to me I'll give you this whole bar of chocolate." And he took a bar of cooking chocolate from the tin.

"What," he said, waving it enticingly at Sandy, "do you say to that?"

"Please," croaked Sandy.

Neil breathed out, broke off a bit of chocolate, and fed it to the dog.

"Do you want any water?" Neil asked.

"I've got some," said Sandy.

Neil bent down to pat the dog, who waved his tail enthusiastically, knowing that he was pleasing his master.

"Do you listen to the wireless much?" Neil asked kindly.

"I can't understand it. I like to talk to Valentina. She tells me about her dogs in . . . in . . ."

"Russia," Neil supplied. He was triumphant. The dog was highly articulate, intelligent, and teachable. His accent was shocking but that could be corrected.

He got up and went back to bed. Sandy stood in the dark, looking at the door and wagging his tail uncertainly. Still, he had enjoyed the chat. He lay down happily and went to sleep.

Next morning Sandy stood by the kitchen door. Ivan, Sophia, and Irena were eating breakfast. Sandy was waiting for his new friend.

As Neil came in, Sandy bounded up and rasped, "Hello, Neil."

The family naturally pretended not to have heard.

"Hello, Sandy," muttered Neil in an embarrassed voice. "Not fair to be rude to the poor little bugger."

"Hrrm," said Irena.

Sandy went into the garden.

As usual, Neil and the rest of them went off to

work. Half an hour later Valentina, on her knees in the hall, heard his car come fast up the drive. He flung open the door, interrupting the chat between Sandy and Valentina, and rushed up the stairs. He ran up the next flight to the attic and began to search. He came down, dragging a large basket. He dumped the basket in the hall, urged the bewildered Sandy into it, and shut the lid. He made Valentina take a handle and help him carry it to the car. With the basket in the back seat, he backed quickly into the road and drove off at top speed. Sandy, in the swaying hamper, moaned gently. At home, Valentina, with her lips set, began to scrub again. "It is not right. It is not just," she said aloud. "And the English are said to be notorious for their fondness for the animals."

Neil drove through London, grinding his gears and cursing. He drove out into Middlesex.

At the shiny office of the P. R. O. for Spanier's pet food he tipped Sandy out. "What's this, Neil?" said the P. R. O.

"Talking dog," said Neil tersely.

"We get one each week, old man," said the P. R. O.

"Not like this," said Neil.

A dazed and startled Sandy went obediently through his paces.

The P. R. O. was appalled. "Remarkable," he said. "I've never seen anything like it. How much do you want?"

"I won't sell the dog for a penny less than two thousand pounds and eight percent," said Neil.

Sandy, sitting at his feet, heard the word *sell*, threw back his head, and howled a long howl of fear and pent-up nervous tension.

"Sensitive little chap, isn't he?" remarked the P. R. O.

"He's as sound as a bell," said Neil quickly. "All this is bound to be a bit of a shock to him."

"You said we were going to see rabbits," howled Sandy. "Rabbits!"

The P. R. O. was shocked. "Well—I'll have to talk to the board," he said.

"I must have a yes or no by four o'clock this afternoon, or it's no go."

"All right, old man," said the P. R. O. soothingly.

As the lid closed again on Sandy, Neil gave him a pat. Sandy, very frightened, whimpered all the way back to Islington, where Neil ejected him into the hall and raced back to his car.

The dog lay trembling where he had been put for half an hour before Valentina could lure him into the kitchen. There she plied him with delicacies and began to ease the story out of him.

"Keep calm, Sandy," she said. "I will take you away with me tomorrow and we will go to Russia. There you will receive great respect and interest and you will be able to live with me always." She went on to outline a radiant future, full of kindly scientists, long rabbity walks through the forests, and no more hostility. Tears of gratitude stood in Sandy's eyes. When Valentina went off with her little basket, he lay down in his and thought about the warm blankets, pine woods, praise, pats, and the kind Valentina.

Events, however, were moving too fast for Sandy, for Neil, for all the Galloways. The accountant appeared that afternoon in Neil's office, two days early, and said he would begin work. Neil headed him off and, sweating, invited him to dinner.

Irena, somewhat annoyed at this unexpected duty and with an idea something nasty was afoot, produced a dinner.

Neil had telephoned Ivan and Sophia, asking them to be at home for the meal. Both scented unpleasantness and refused to come. Belinda also refused on the grounds that she was going to visit her mother. So Neil had to face the accountant, a thin, decent-looking man called Nevers, with no backing but the huffy Irena, thwarted, because of the shortness of time, from producing any extraordinary surprises.

Small wonder if, lacking other allies, Neil embraced the bottle.

They were sitting in the living room drinking their coffee. Neil, in spite of Irena's unobtrusive efforts to stop him, was also drinking brandy.

The doors of the kitchen and living room had been left open. Sandy trotted in and lay down under the piano. Irena glanced at him, making a mental note to eject him when the time came to do it naturally. Nevers spotted him.

"Nice dog," he said. "He looks very intelligent."

Sandy's tail flopped feebly up and down on the parquet, but he continued to stare at Neil with his huge brown eyes.

"He seems to understand," Nevers went on.

"He's a nice animal," Irena said. "Have you got a dog?"

"Yes, a Labrador," said Nevers. "He's getting old now, poor old thing. My wife and I will be heartbroken when he goes."

Sandy, overcome by emotion, began to whine.

"Something wrong with him?" Nevers inquired.

"He sometimes does that," Irena said smoothly and turned the conversation to a discussion of the neighborhood. "So very nice and *mixed*," she said. "So unsnobbish—"

Sandy's whine grew louder. "Sandy! Whatever is the *matter*?" Irena said crossly and, as she realized a moment later, very unwisely.

As she began to speak again, Sandy howled long and hard. "Neil's going to sell me and send me away," he keened.

Nevers started and almost dropped his coffee cup. He sat bolt upright and stared at Sandy.

"You're going to *what*?" Irena asked Neil with a hard edge to her voice.

"Give me awa-a-ay, give me awa-a-y," moaned Sandy.

"Oh, my God," said Neil, standing up and swaying in the middle of the room with his hands over his ears.

Irena felt a strange emotion growing in her. She fell on her strong knees beside Sandy and said in his ear, "No, no, Sandy. We won't give you to anyone else."

"I'm going with Valentina," came Sandy's muffled rasp.

"That's all right, Sandy—" said Irena.

"Shut up," said Neil Galloway drunkenly. "The dog's going."

Nevers stood up. "Perhaps I'd better say goodnight," he said pleasantly.

No one took any notice.

"He's got to get the money," Sandy told Irena. "Eight-underd pounds."

"What!" said Irena. Pulling herself together she

said, "Well. We can sort it all out later. Come out with me and have some food in the kitchen, Sandy. And don't worry."

She led Sandy out. Nevers, still in a leaving position, said, "What a remarkable animal," to Neil.

"Try living with the bastard," Neil said thickly.

Irena returned. "I've given him something to eat," she said. "Poor old Sandy." She looked expectantly at Nevers, who said, "I must be going, Mrs. Galloway. Thank you for a delightful meal—and the interesting experience—I suppose you're not having me on?" he said to Neil.

Neil muttered something. "Well, well," said Nevers. He walked out into the hall and collected his hat. Irena followed him.

There was the sound of paws thudding against the kitchen door and mingled howls and shouts. Irena tried to say good-bye to Nevers, who attempted to reply. The howling and growling shouts continued. Irena, suddenly not caring at all and full of rebellious spirit, shrugged and said, "Oh, hell, I'll let him out."

She opened the kitchen door and Sandy fell out. She picked him up. Nevers moved toward the door. Irena, carrying Sandy, followed. "He fights Belinda on the sofa, like you do with Piotr," remarked the dog. Irena flushed, gave a groan, and her face sagged. "Well, well," she said. "You are an observant dog."

Neil appeared swaying in the living room doorway. Nevers stood on the step, about to leave.

"He's going to get money for me," wailed Sandy and began to howl again. Irena put him down.

Nevers lifted his hat to Irena and smiled. "Thank you again."

"I'm sorry about all this," said Irena.

Sandy ran over to Neil and said, "You took money. Belinda said so. You want to sell me-e-e-e-e." His howl appeared to the listeners to be endless.

Irena gave a hopeless groan. Nevers lifted his eyebrows and said directly to Irena, "I'm so sorry."

Neil bounded forward, dropping his brandy glass, which splintered on the floor.

"You damned lying dog," he screamed.

"You're selling me-e-e-e-e," Sandy moaned, standing at his feet and looking up at him.

"You bastard," shouted Neil and kicked Sandy in the ribs, hard. Sandy went sprawling. Neil went after him and kicked him again and again. "Bastard," he was shouting. "Bastard, bastard, bastard."

Nevers ran in and pulled Neil away. He dragged him back into the living room and dropped him on the sofa. Irena was crouching over Sandy in the hall. Nevers dropped onto his knees beside her. Sandy was howling and gasping.

"My God, my God," said Irena.

"We'd better get him to the R.S.P.C.A.," said Nevers. The dog bit him as he picked him up.

"Will your husband be all right?" Nevers asked as he carried Sandy to his car.

"I expect so," said Irena.

Sandy lay motionless in the back of the car with Irena beside him. The air came through his lips with a little whistling sound. Irena patted him and talked to him on the drive. As they drew up outside the R.S.P.C.A., Sandy gave a moan and died.

All four Galloways were still awake at five the next morning, sitting in the living room, drinking tea, dropping ash on the parquet, faces pale, hair disheveled, clothes awry.

Ivan and Sophia had come in while Irena was talking to Neil. The story of the embezzlements and the death of Sandy had been told. Recriminations began, sums of money were added up, extravagances laid at each other's doors. Out came the story of Samantha's pregnancy, secretly terminated with the help of kindly old Doctor Nugent and paid for by Samuel, Michael, and James. The argument, a mélange of cars, bills, lovers, mortgages, selfish children, and irresponsible parents, went on for what seemed an eternity, a timeless world in which memories of the past were as fresh as if they were yesterday's news and predictions about the future seemed unalterably true.

The family went to bed stale-mouthed and sick.

At 11 A.M., they were seated grubbily in the living room, drinking coffee. The doorbell rang. Irena went to answer it.

On the step was a hard-faced woman with a large wicker shopping basket over her arm. Her eyes widened at the sight of her usually impeccable neighbor frowsy in a toweling wrapper.

"I believe," she said coldly, "that you have been letting your dog out without proper control again. These, I think, are yours."

She handed the basket over to Irena. It contained four beady-eyed black puppies. "I should be grateful if I could have the basket back in due course," she said.

Irena took the basket into the living room. "These," she said, "are four puppies of Sandy's. Their mother was his mother, too."

No one spoke. Finally Neil passed his hand across his puffy eyes. "Get rid of them before they start to sing 'God Save the Queen,'" he said.

"I think I'll breed them," said Irena, "and see what happens."

"Irena," said Neil, "those dogs are a menace."

Irena merely smiled and tipped the basket onto the shining parquet floor. Sandy's puppies rolled about, squeaking, sniffling, and tumbling over each other.

The Galloways watched them silently.

The Drowned Giant

By J. G. Ballard

This strange narrative about what happens when the body of a giant man washes ashore near an unnamed town is told so matter-of-factly that you might almost forget how fantastic the story is. You can take it, as I do, as an allegory of the disintegration of the spirit, or give it a number of other interpretations— including one that says this is simply and exactly what would *happen if such a gigantic phenomenon were to appear on our shores.*

On the morning after the storm the body of a drowned giant was washed ashore on the beach five miles to the northwest of the city. The first news of its arrival was brought by a nearby farmer and subsequently confirmed by the local newspaper reporters and the police. Despite this the majority of people, I among them, remained skeptical, but the return of more and more eyewitnesses attesting to the vast size of the giant was finally too much for our curiosity. The library where my colleagues and I were carrying out our research was almost deserted when we set off for the coast shortly after two o'clock, and throughout the day people continued to leave their offices and shops as accounts of the giant circulated around the city.

By the time we reached the dunes above the beach, a substantial crowd had gathered, and we could see the body lying in the shallow water two hundred yards away. At first the estimates of its size seemed greatly exaggerated. It was then at low tide, and almost all the giant's body was exposed, but he appeared to be little larger than a basking shark. He lay on his back with his arms at his sides, in an attitude of repose, as if asleep on the mirror of wet sand, the reflection of his blanched skin fading as the water receded. In the clear sunlight his body glistened like the white plumage of a seabird.

Puzzled by this spectacle and dissatisfied with the matter-of-fact explanations of the crowd, my friends and I stepped down from the dunes onto the shingle. Everyone seemed reluctant to approach the giant, but half an hour later two fishermen in wading boots walked out across the sand. As their diminutive figures neared the recumbent body, a sudden hubbub of conversation broke out among the spectators. The two men were completely dwarfed by the giant. Although his heels were partly submerged in the sand, the feet rose to at least twice the fishermen's height, and we immediately realized that this drowned leviathan had the mass and dimensions of the largest sperm whale.

Three fishing smacks had arrived on the scene and with keels raised remained a quarter of a mile offshore, the crews watching from the bows. Their discretion deterred the spectators on the shore from wading out across the sand. Impatiently everyone stepped down from the dunes and waited on the single slopes, eager for a closer view. Around the margins of the figure the sand had been washed away, forming a hollow, as if the giant had fallen out of the sky. The two fishermen were standing between the immense plinths of the feet, waving to us like tourists among the columns of some water-lapped temple on the Nile. For a moment I feared that the giant was merely asleep and might suddenly stir and clap his heels together, but his glazed eyes stared skyward, unaware of the minuscule replicas of himself between his feet.

The fishermen then began a circuit of the corpse, strolling past the long white flanks of the legs. After a pause to examine the fingers of the supine hand, they disappeared from sight between the arm and chest, then re-emerged to survey the head, shielding their eyes as they gazed up at its Grecian profile. The shallow forehead, straight high-bridged nose and curling lips reminded me of a Roman copy of Praxiteles, and the elegantly formed cartouches of the nostrils emphasized the resemblance to sculpture.

Abruptly there was a shout from the crowd, and a hundred arms pointed to the sea. With a start I saw that one of the fishermen had climbed onto the giant's chest and was now strolling about and signaling to the shore. There was a roar of surprise and triumph from the crowd, lost in a rushing avalanche of shingle as everyone surged forward across the sand.

As we approached the recumbent figure, which was lying in a pool of water the size of a field, our excited chatter fell away again, subdued by the huge physical dimensions of this dead colossus. He was stretched out at a slight angle to the shore, his legs carried nearer the beach, and this foreshortening had disguised his true length. Despite the two fishermen standing on his abdomen, the crowd formed itself into a wide circle, groups of people tentatively advancing toward the hands and feet.

My companions and I walked around the seaward side of the giant, whose hips and thorax towered above us like the hull of a stranded ship. His pearl-colored skin, distended by immersion in salt water, masked the contours of the enormous muscles and tendons. We passed below the left knee, which was flexed slightly, threads of damp seaweed clinging to its sides. Draped loosely across the midriff, and preserving a tenuous propriety, was a shawl of heavy open-weave material, bleached to a pale yellow by the water. A strong odor of brine came from the garment as it steamed in the sun, mingled with the sweet, potent scent of the giant's skin.

We stopped by his shoulder and gazed up at the motionless profile. The lips were parted slightly, the open eye cloudy and occluded, as if injected with some blue milky liquid, but the delicate arches of the nostrils and eyebrows invested the face with an ornate charm that belied the brutish power of the chest and shoulders.

The ear was suspended in midair over our heads like a sculptured doorway. As I raised my hand to touch the pendulous lobe, someone appeared over the edge of the forehead and shouted down at me. Startled by this apparition, I stepped back, and then saw that a group of youths had climbed up onto the face and were jostling each other in and out of the orbits.

People were now clambering all over the giant, whose reclining arms provided a double stairway. From the palms they walked along the forearms to the elbows and then crawled over the distended belly of the biceps to the flat promenade of the pectoral muscles which covered the upper half of the smooth hairless chest. From here they climbed up onto the face, hand over hand along the lips and nose, or forayed down the abdomen to meet others who had straddled the ankles and were patrolling the twin columns of the thighs.

We continued our circuit through the crowd and stopped to examine the outstretched right hand. A small pool of water lay in the palm, like the residue of another world, now being kicked away by the people ascending the arm. I tried to read the palm lines that grooved the skin, searching for some clue to the giant's character, but the distention of the tissues had almost obliterated them, carrying away all trace of the giant's identity and his last tragic predicament. The huge muscles and wristbones of the hand seemed to deny any sensitivity to their owner, but the delicate flexion of the fingers and the well-tended nails, each cut symmetrically to within six inches of the quick, argued a certain refinement of temperament, illustrated in the Grecian features of the face, on which the townsfolk were now sitting like flies.

One youth was even standing, arms wavering at his sides, on the very tip of the nose, shouting down at his companions, but the face of the giant still retained its massive composure.

Returning to the shore, we sat down on the shingle and watched the continuous stream of people arriving from the city. Some six or seven fishing boats had collected offshore, and their crews waded in through the shallow water for a closer look at this enormous storm catch. Later a party of police appeared and made a half-hearted attempt to cordon off the beach, but after walking up to the recumbent figure, any such thoughts left their minds, and they went off together with bemused backward glances.

An hour later there were a thousand people present on the beach, at least two hundred of them standing or sitting on the giant, crowded along his arms and legs or circulating in a ceaseless melee across his chest and stomach. A large gang of youths occupied the head, toppling each other off the cheeks and sliding down the smooth planes of the jaw. Two or three straddled the nose, and another crawled into one of the nostrils, from which he emitted barking noises like a demented dog.

That afternoon the police returned and cleared a way through the crowd for a party of scientific experts—authorities on gross anatomy and marine biology—from the university. The gang of youths and most of the people on the giant climbed down, leaving behind a few hardy spirits perched on the tips of the toes and on the forehead. The experts strode around the giant, heads nodding in vigorous consultation, preceded by the policemen who pushed back the press of spectators. When they reached the outstretched hand, the experts hastily demurred.

After they returned to the shore, the crowd once more climbed onto the giant, and was in full possession when we left at five o'clock, covering the arms and legs like a dense flock of gulls sitting on the corpse of a large fish.

I next visited the beach three days later. My friends at the library had returned to their work, and delegated to me the task of keeping the giant under observation and preparing a report. Perhaps they sensed my particular interest in the case, and it was certainly true that I was eager to return to the beach. There was nothing necrophilic about this, for to all intents the giant was still alive for me, indeed more alive than many of the people watching him. What I found so fascinating was partly his immense scale, the huge volumes of space occupied by his arms and legs, which seemed to confirm the identity of my own miniature limbs, but above all, the mere categorical fact of his existence. Whatever else in our lives might be open to doubt, the giant, dead or alive, existed in an absolute sense, providing a glimpse into a world of similar absolutes of which we spectators on the beach were such imperfect and puny copies.

When I arrived at the beach the crowd was considerably smaller, and some two or three hundred people sat on the shingle, picnicking and watching the groups of visitors who walked out across the sand. The successive tides had carried the giant nearer the shore, swinging his head and shoulders toward the beach, so that he seemed doubly to gain in size, his huge body dwarfing the fishing boats beached beside his feet. The uneven contours of the beach had pushed his spine into a slight arch, expanding his chest and tilting back the head, forcing him into a more expressly heroic posture. The combined effects of seawater and the tumefaction of the tissues had given the face a sleeker and less youthful look. Although the vast proportions of the features made it impossible to assess the age and character of the giant, on my previous visit his classically modeled mouth and nose suggested that he had been a young man of discreet and modest temper. Now, however, he appeared to be at least in early middle age. The puffy cheeks, thicker nose and temples and narrowing eyes gave him a look of well-fed maturity that even now hinted at a growing corruption to come.

This accelerated postmortem development of the giant's character, as if the latent elements of his personality had gained sufficient momentum during his life to discharge themselves in a brief final résumé, continued to fascinate me. It marked the beginning of the giant's surrender to that all-demanding system of time in which the rest of humanity finds itself, and of which, like the million twisted ripples of a fragmented whirlpool, our finite lives are the concluding products. I took up my position on the shingle directly opposite the giant's head, from where I could see the new arrivals and the children clambering over the legs and arms.

Among the morning's visitors were a number of men in leather jackets and cloth caps, who peered up critically at the giant with a professional eye, pacing out his dimensions and making rough calculations in the sand with spars of driftwood. I assumed them to be from the public works department and other municipal bodies, no doubt wondering how to dispose of this monster.

Several rather more smartly attired individuals, circus proprietors and the like, also appeared on the scene, and strolled slowly around the giant, hands in the pockets of their long overcoats, saying nothing to one another. Evidently its bulk was too great even for their matchless enterprise. After they had gone, the children continued to run up and down the arms and legs, and the youths wrestled with each other over the supine face, the damp sand from their feet covering the white skin.

The following day I deliberately postponed my visit until the late afternoon, and when I arrived there were fewer than fifty or sixty people sitting on the shingle. The giant had been carried still closer to the shore, and was now little more than seventy-five yards away, his feet crushing the palisade of a rotting breakwater. The slope of the firmer sand tilted his body toward the sea, the bruised, swollen face averted in an almost conscious gesture. I sat down on a large metal winch which had been shackled to a concrete caisson above the shingle, and looked down at the recumbent figure.

His blanched skin had now lost its pearly translucence and was spattered with dirty sand which replaced that washed away by the night tide. Clumps of seaweed filled the intervals between the fingers and a collection of litter and cuttlebones lay in the crevices below the hips and knees. But despite this, and the continuous thickening of his features, the giant still retained his magnificent Homeric stature. The enormous breadth of the shoulders, and the huge columns of the arms and legs, still carried the figure into another dimension, and the giant seemed a more authentic image of one of the drowned Argonauts or heroes of the *Odyssey* than the conventional portrait previously in my mind.

I stepped down onto the sand, and walked between the pools of water toward the giant. Two small boys were sitting in the well of the ear, and at the far end a solitary youth stood perched high on one of the toes, surveying me as I approached. As I had hoped when delaying my visit, no one else paid any attention to me, and the people on the shore remained huddled beneath their coats.

The giant's supine right hand was covered with broken shells and sand, in which a score of footprints were visible. The rounded bulk of the hip towered above me, cutting off all sight of the sea. The sweetly acrid odor I had noticed before was now more pungent, and through the opaque skin I could see the serpentine coils of congealed blood vessels. However repellent it seemed, this ceaseless metamorphosis, a macabre life-in-death, alone permitted me to set foot on the corpse.

Using the jutting thumb as a stair rail, I climbed up onto the palm and began my ascent. The skin was harder than I expected, barely yielding to my weight. Quickly I walked up the sloping forearm and the bulging balloon of the biceps. The face of the drowned giant loomed to my right, the cavernous nostrils and huge flanks of the cheeks like the cone of some freakish volcano.

Safely rounding the shoulder, I stepped out onto the broad promenade of the chest, across which the bony ridges of the rib cage lay like huge rafters. The white skin was dappled by the darkening bruises of countless footprints, in which the patterns of individual heel marks were clearly visible. Someone had built a small sand castle on the center of the sternum, and I climbed onto this partly demolished structure to get a better view of the face.

The two children had now scaled the ear and were pulling themselves into the right orbit, whose blue globe, completely occluded by some milk-colored fluid, gazed sightlessly past their miniature forms. Seen obliquely from below, the face was devoid of all grace and repose, the drawn mouth and raised chin propped up by gigantic slings of muscles resembling the torn prow of a colossal wreck. For the first time I became aware of the extremity of this last physical agony of the giant, no less painful for his unawareness of the collapsing musculature and tissues. The absolute isolation of the ruined figure, cast like an abandoned ship upon the empty shore, almost out of sound of the waves, transformed his face into a mask of exhaustion and helplessness.

As I stepped forward, my foot sank into a trough of soft tissue, and a gust of fetid gas blew through an aperture between the ribs. Retreating from the fouled air, which hung like a cloud over my head, I turned toward the sea to clear my lungs. To my surprise I saw that the giant's left hand had been amputated.

I stared with shocked bewilderment at the blackening stump, while the solitary youth reclining on his aerial perch a hundred feet away surveyed me with a sanguinary eye.

This was only the first of a sequence of depredations. I spent the following two days in the library, for some reason reluctant to visit the shore, aware that I had probably witnessed the approaching end of a magnificent illusion. When I next crossed the dunes and set foot on the shingle, the giant was little more than twenty yards away, and with this close proximity to the rough pebbles all traces had vanished of the magic which once surrounded his distant wave-washed form. Despite his immense size, the bruises and dirt that covered his body made him appear merely human in scale, his vast dimensions only increasing his vulnerability.

His right hand and foot had been removed, dragged up the slope and trundled away by cart. After questioning the small group of people huddled by the breakwater, I gathered that a fertilizer company and a cattlefood manufacturer were responsible.

The giant's remaining foot rose into the air, a steel hawser fixed to the large toe, evidently in preparation for the following day. The surrounding beach had been disturbed by a score of workmen, and deep ruts marked the ground where the hands and foot had been hauled away. A dark brackish fluid leaked from the stumps, and stained the sand and the white cones of the cuttlefish. As I walked down the shingle I noticed that a number of jocular slogans, swastikas and other signs had been cut into the gray skin, as if the mutilation of this motionless colossus had released a sudden flood of repressed spite. The lobe of one of the ears was pierced by a spear of timber, and a small fire had burned out in the center of the chest, blackening the surrounding skin. The fine wood ash was still being scattered by the wind.

A foul smell enveloped the cadaver, the undisguisable signature of putrefaction, which had at last driven away the usual gathering of youths. I returned to the shingle and climbed up onto the winch. The giant's swollen cheeks had now almost closed his eyes, drawing the lips back in a monumental gape. The once straight Grecian nose had been twisted and flattened, stamped into the ballooning face by countless heels.

When I visited the beach the following day I found, almost with relief, that the head had been removed.

Some weeks elapsed before I made my next journey to the beach, and by then the human likeness I had noticed earlier had vanished again. On close inspection the recumbent thorax and abdomen were unmistakably manlike, but as each of the limbs was chopped off, first at the knee and elbow, and then at shoulder and thigh, the carcass resembled that of any headless sea animal—whale or whale shark. With this loss of identity, and the few traces of personality that had clung tenuously to the figure, the interest of the spectators expired, and the foreshore was deserted except for an elderly beachcomber and the watchman sitting in the doorway of the contractor's hut.

A loose wooden scaffolding had been erected around the carcass, from which a dozen ladders swung in the wind, and the surrounding sand was littered with coils of rope, long metal-handled knives and grappling irons, the pebbles oily with blood and pieces of bone and skin.

I nodded to the watchman, who regarded me dourly over his brazier of burning coke. The whole area was pervaded by the pungent smell of huge squares of blubber being simmered in a vat behind the hut.

Both the thighbones had been removed, with the assistance of a small crane draped in the gauzelike fabric which had once covered the waist of the giant, and the open sockets gaped like barn doors. The upper arms, collarbones, and pudenda had likewise been dispatched. What remained of the skin over the thorax and abdomen had been marked out in parallel strips with a tarbrush, and the first five or six sections had been pared away from the midriff, revealing the great arch of the rib cage.

As I left, a flock of gulls wheeled down from the sky and alighted on the beach, picking at the stained sand with ferocious cries.

Several months later, when the news of his arrival had been generally forgotten, various pieces of the body of the dismembered giant began to reappear all over the city. Most of these were bones, which the fertilizer manufacturers had found too difficult to crush, and their massive size, and the huge tendons and disks of cartilage attached to their joints, immediately identified them. For some reason, these disembodied fragments seemed better to convey the essence of the giant's original magnificence than the bloated appendages that had been subsequently amputated. As I looked across the road at the premises of the largest wholesale merchants in the meat market, I recognized the two enormous thighbones on either side of the doorway. They towered over the porters' heads like the threatening megaliths of some primitive druidical religion, and I had a sudden vision of the giant climbing to his knees upon these bare bones and striding away through the streets of the city, picking up the scattered fragments of himself on his return journey to the sea.

A few days later I saw the left humerus lying in the entrance to one of the shipyards. In the same week the mummified right hand was exhibited on a carnival float during the annual pageant of the guilds.

The lower jaw, typically, found its way to the museum of natural history. The remainder of the skull has disappeared, but is probably still lurking in the waste grounds or private gardens of the city—quite recently, while sailing down the river, I noticed two ribs of the giant forming a decorative arch in a waterside garden, possibly confused with the jawbones of a whale. A large square of tanned and tattooed skin, the size of an Indian blanket, forms a back cloth to the dolls and masks in a novelty shop near the amusment park, and I have no doubt that elsewhere in the city, in the hotels or golf clubs, the mummified nose or ears of the giant hang from the wall above a fireplace. As for the immense pizzle, this ends its days in the freak museum of a circus which travels up and down the Northwest. This monumental apparatus, stunning in its proportions and sometime potency, occupies a complete booth to itself. The irony is that it is wrongly identified as that of a whale, and indeed most people, even those who first saw him cast up on the shore after the storm, now remember the giant, if at all, as a large sea beast.

The remainder of the skeleton, stripped of all flesh, still rests on the seashore, the clutter of bleached ribs like the timbers of a derelict ship. The contractor's hut, the crane and scaffolding have been removed, and the sand being driven into the bay along the coast has buried the pelvis and backbone. In the winter the high curved bones are deserted, battered by the breaking waves, but in the summer they provide an excellent perch for the sea-wearying gulls.

Inside

By Carol Carr

Carol Carr is the author of Look, You Think
You've Got Troubles, *one of the funniest and
most reprinted science-fiction stories of the past
ten years. Yet I've always preferred her short,
biting fantasy about a woman who awoke to
find herself in a mist-shrouded house that
added rooms and grew day by day . . . until it
threatened to grow too much.*

*T*he house was a jigsaw puzzle of many
dreams. It could not exist in reality and, dimly, the
girl knew this. But she wandered its changing halls
and corridors each day with a mild, floating interest.
In the six months she had lived here the house had
grown rapidly, spinning out attics, basements, and
strangely geometric alcoves with translucent white
curtains that never moved. Since she believed she had
been reborn in this house, she never questioned her
presence in it.

Her bedroom came first. When she woke to find
herself in it she was not frightened, and she was only
vaguely apprehensive when she discovered that the
door opened to blackness. She was not curious and
she was not hungry. She spent most of the first day

in her four-poster bed looking at the heavy, flowered material that framed the bay window. Outside the window was a yellow-gray mist. She was not disturbed; the mist was a comfort. Although she experienced no joy, she knew that she loved this room and the small bathroom that was an extension of it.

On the second day she opened the carved doors of the mahogany wardrobe and removed a quilted dressing gown. It was a little large and the sleeves partially covered her hands. Her fingers, long and pale, reached out uncertainly from the edge of the material. She didn't want to open the bedroom door again but felt that she should; if there was something outside to discover, it, too, would belong to her.

She turned the doorknob and stepped out into a narrow hall, paneled, like the wardrobe in her room, in carved mahogany. There were no pictures and no carpet. The polished wood of the floor felt cool against her bare feet. When she had walked the full distance to the end and touched a wall, she turned and walked to the other end. The hall was very long, and there were no new rooms leading from it.

When she got back to her bedroom she noticed a large desk in the corner near the window. She didn't remember a desk but she accepted it as she accepted the rest. She looked out and saw that the mist was still there. She felt protected.

Later that afternoon she began to be hungry. She opened various drawers of the desk and found them empty except for a dusty tin of chocolates. She ate slowly and filled a glass with water from the bathroom sink and drank it all at once. Her mouth tasted bad; she wished she had a toothbrush.

On the second day she had wandered as far as the house allowed her to. Then she slept, woke in a drowsy, numb state, and slept again.

On the third day she found stairs, three flights. They led her down to a kitchen, breakfast area, and pantry. Unlike her room, the kitchen was tiled and modern. She ate a Swiss cheese sandwich and drank a glass of milk. The trip back to her room tired her and she fell asleep at once.

The house continued to grow. Bedrooms appeared, some like her own, some modern, some a confusion of periods and styles. A toothbrush and a small tube of toothpaste appeared in her medicine cabinet. In each of the bedrooms she found new clothes and wore them in the order of their discovery.

She began to awaken in the morning with a feeling of anticipation. Would she find a chandeliered dining room or perhaps an enclosed porch whose windows looked out on the mist?

At the end of a month the house contained eighteen bedrooms, three parlors, a library, dining room, ballroom, music room, sewing room, a basement, and two attics.

Then the people came. One night she awoke to their laughter somewhere beyond her window. She was furious at the invasion but comforted herself with the thought that they were outside. She would bolt the downstairs door, and even if the mist disappeared she would not look. But she couldn't help hearing them talk and laugh. She strained to catch the words and hated herself for trying. This was *her* house. She stuffed cotton into her ears and felt shut out rather than shut in, which angered her even more.

The house stopped growing. The mist cleared and the sun came out. She looked through her window and saw a lake made up of many narrow branches, its surfaces covered with a phosphorescent sparkle like a skin of dirty green sequins. She saw no one—the intruders came late at night, dozens of them, judging from the sound they made.

She lost weight. She looked in the mirror and found her hair dull, her cheeks drawn. She began to wander the house at odd hours. Her dreams were haunted by the voices outside, the splash of water, and, worst of all, the endless laughter. What would these strangers do if she suddenly appeared at the doorway in her quilted robe and demanded that they leave? If she said nothing but hammered a "No Trespass" sign to the oak tree? What if they just stood there, staring at her, laughing?

She continued to wander. There were no new rooms, but she discovered hidden alcoves and passageways that connected bedroom to bedroom, library to kitchen. She used these passageways over and over again, avoiding the main halls.

Now when she woke, it was with a feeling of dread. Had any of them got in during the night, in spite of her precautions? She found carpenters' tools in a closet and nailed the windows shut. It took weeks to finish the job, and then she realized she had forgotten the windows in the basement. That part of the house frightened her and she put off going down. But when the voices at night began to sound more and more distinct, when she imagined that they were voices she recognized, she knew that she had no choice.

The basement was dark and damp. She could find

no objects to account for the shadows on the walls. There was not enough light to work by, and when she finished, she knew she had done badly. If they really wanted to come in, these crooked nails would not stop them.

The next morning she found that the house had a new wing of three bedrooms. They were smaller than those in the rest of the house and more cheaply furnished.

She never knew exactly when the servants moved in. She saw the first one, the cook, when she walked into the kitchen one morning. The woman, middle-aged, and heavy, wearing a black uniform with white apron, was taking eggs from the refrigerator.

"How would you like them, madam?"

Before she could reply, the doorbell rang. A butler appeared.

"No, don't answer it!" He continued to walk. "Please—"

"I beg your pardon, madam. I am partially deaf. Would you repeat your statement?"

She screamed: *"Do not answer the door."*

"Scrambled, fried, poached?" said the cook.

"It may be the postman," said the butler.

"Would madam like to see today's menu? Does madam plan to have guests this evening?" The housekeeper was dark and wiry. She hardly moved her lips but her words were clear.

"Some nice cinnamon toast, I think," the cook said, and she placed two slices of bread in the toaster.

"If you're having twelve to dinner, madam, I would suggest the lace cloth," said the housekeeper.

The doorbell was still ringing. It wouldn't stop. She ran to the stairs, toward the safety of her room.

"Madam?" said the cook, the housekeeper, the butler.

That night they came at sunset. She climbed into bed and drew the covers up around her, but still she could hear their laughter, rising and falling. The water made splashing sounds. She pulled the covers over her head and burrowed beneath them.

A new sound reached her and she threw off the covers, straining to hear. They were downstairs, in the dining room. She could make out the clink of silverware against dishes, the kind of laughter and talking that came up at her from the water. The house was alive with a chattering and clattering she could not endure. She would confront them, explain that this was her house; they would have to leave. Then the servants.

She went down the stairs slowly, rehearsing the exact words she would use. When she reached the ballroom floor she stopped for a second, then crossed it to the open doors of the dining room. She flattened herself against the wall and looked inside.

There were twelve of them, as the housekeeper had suggested—and she knew every one.

Her husband, bald, bold, and precise: "I told her, 'Go ahead and jump; you're not scaring me.' And she jumped. The only brave thing she ever did."

Her mother, dry as a twig, with dead eyes: "I told her it was a sin—but she never listened to me, never."

A friend: "She didn't seem to feel anything. When other people laughed she always looked serious, as if she was mulling it over to find the joke."

"She used to laugh when she was very small. Then she stopped."

"She was a bore."

"She was a sparrow."

"She was a failure. Everyone knew. When she found out for herself, she jumped."

"Was it from a bridge? I was always curious about that."

"Yes. They found her floating on the surface, staring into the sun like some would-be Ophelia." Her husband smiled and wiped his lips with a napkin. "I don't think I'll recommend this place. I've got a stomachache."

The others agreed. They all had stomachaches.

The guests returned, night after night, but each night it was a different group. Always she knew them and always she watched as they ate. When the last party left, joking about the food being poisoned, she was alone. She didn't have to dismiss the servants; they were gone the next day. The yellow-gray mist surrounded her windows again, and for the first time she could remember, she laughed.

The Old Folks

BY JAMES E. GUNN

Here is a deceptively calm story by James E. Gunn, author of (among numerous others) the novel on which the television series The Immortal *was based. In the present story, Gunn tells of a young family's visit to a community for an older generation. I suppose you might call this a "generation gap" story . . . but that would be rather an understatement.*

They had been traveling in the dusty car all day, the last few miles in the heat of the Florida summer. Not far behind were the Sunshine State Parkway, Orange Grove, and Winter Hope, but according to the road map the end of the trip was near.

John almost missed the sign that said, "Sunset Acres, Next Right," but the red Volkswagen slowed and turned and slowed again. Now another sign marked the beginning of the town proper: SUNSET ACRES, Restricted Senior Citizens, Minimum Age—65, Maximum Speed—20.

As the car passed the sign, the whine of the tires announced that the pavement had changed from concrete to brick.

Johnny bounced in the back seat, mingling the

squeak of the springs with the music of the tires, and shouted above the engine's protest at second gear, "Mommy—Daddy, are we there yet? Are we there?"

His mother turned to look at him. The wind from the open window whipped her short hair. She smiled. "Soon now," she said. Her voice was excited, too.

They passed through a residential section where the white frame houses with their sharp roofs sat well back from the street, and the velvet lawns reached from red-brick sidewalks to broad porches that spread like skirts around two or three sides of the houses.

At each intersection the streets dipped to channel the rain water and to enforce the speed limit at twenty m.p.h. or slower. The names of the streets were chiseled into the curbs, and the incisions were painted black: Osage, Cottonwood, Antelope, Meadowlark, Prairie. . . .

The Volkswagen hummed along the brick streets, alone. The streets were empty, and so, it seemed, were the houses; the white-curtained windows stared senilely into the Florida sun, and the swings on the porches creaked in the Florida breeze, but the architecture and the town were all Kansas—and the Kansas of fifty years ago, at that.

Then they reached the square, and John pulled the car to a stop alongside the curb. Here was the center of town—a block of greensward edged with beds of pansies and petunias and geraniums. In the center of the square was a massive two-story red brick building. A square tower reached even taller. The tower had a big clock set into its face. The heavy black hands pointed at three thirty-two.

Stone steps marched up the front of the building toward oak doors twice the height of a man. Around the edges of the buildings were iron benches painted white. On the benches the old men sat in the sun, their eyes shut, their hands folded across canes.

From somewhere behind the brick building came the sound of a brass band—the full, rich mixture of trumpet and trombone and sousaphone, of tuba and timpani and big bass drum.

Unexpectedly, as they sat in the car looking at the scene out of another era and another land, a tall black shape rolled silently past them. John turned his head quickly to look at it. A thin cab in the middle sloped toward spoked wheels at each end, like the front ends of two cars stuck together. An old woman in a wide-brimmed hat sat upright beside the driver. From her high window she frowned at the little foreign car, and then her vehicle passed down the street.

"That was an old electric!" John said. "I didn't know they were making them again."

From the back seat Johnny said, "When are we going to get to Grammy's?"

"Soon," his mother said. "If you're going to ask the way to Buffalo Street, you'd better ask," she said to John. "It's too hot to sit here in the car."

John opened the door and extracted himself from the damp socket of the bucket seat. He stood for a moment beside the baked metal of the car and looked up each side of the street. The oomp-pah-pah of the band was louder now and the yeasty smell of baking bread dilated his nostrils, but the whole scene struck him as unreal somehow, as if this all were a stage setting and a man could walk behind the buildings and find that the backs were unpainted canvas and raw wood.

"Well?" Sally said.

John shook his head and walked around the front of the car. The first store sold hardware. In the small front window were crowbars and wooden-handled claw hammers and three kegs of blue nails; one of the kegs had a metal scoop stuck into the nails at the top. In one corner of the window was a hand mower, its handle varnished wood, its metal wheels and reel blue, except where the spokes had been touched with red and yellow paint and the curved reel had been sharpened to a silver line.

The interior of the store was dark; John could not tell whether anyone was inside.

Next to it was "Tyler's General Store," and John stepped inside onto sawdust. Before his eyes adjusted from the Sunshine State's proudest asset, he smelled the pungent sawdust. The odor was mingled with others—the vinegar and spice of pickles and the ripeness of cheese and a sweet-sour smell that he could not identify.

Into his returning vision the faces swam first— the pale faces of the old people, framed in white hair, relieved from the anonymity of age only by the way in which bushy eyebrows sprouted or a moustache was trimmed or wrinkles carved the face. Then he saw the rest of the store and the old people. Some of them were sitting in scarred oak chairs with rounded backs near a black potbellied stove. The room was cool; after a moment John realized that the stove was producing a cold breeze.

One old man with a drooping white moustache

was leaning over from the barrel he sat on to cut a slice of cheese from the big wheel on the counter. A tall man with an apron over his shirt and trousers and his shirt sleeves hitched up with rubber bands came from behind the counter, moving his bald head with practiced ease among the dangling sausages.

"Son," he said, "I reckon you lost your way. Made the wrong turn off the highway, I warrant. Heading for Winter Hope or beyond and mistook yourself. You just head back out how you come in and—"

"Is this Sunset Acres?" John said.

The old man with the yellow slice of cheese in his hand said in a thin voice, "Yep. No use thinking you can stay, though. Thirty-five or forty years too soon. That's what!" His sudden laughter came out in a cackle.

The others joined in, like a superannuated Greek chorus, "Can't stay!"

"I'm looking for Buffalo Street," John said. "We're going to visit the Plummers." He paused and then added, "They're my wife's parents."

The storekeeper tucked his thumbs into the straps of his apron. "That's different. Everybody knows the Plummers. Three blocks north of the square. Can't miss it."

"Thank you," John said, nodding, and backed into the sunshine.

The interrupted murmur of conversation began again, broken briefly by laughter.

"Three blocks north of the square," he said as he inserted himself back in the car.

He started the motor, shifted into first, and turned the corner. As he passed the general store he thought he saw white faces peering out of the darkness, but they might have been feather pillows hanging in the window.

In front of the town hall an old man jerked in his sleep as the car passed. Another opened his eyes and frowned. A third shook his cane in their general direction. Beyond, a thin woman in a lavender shawl was holding an old man by the shoulder as if to tell him that she was done with the shopping and it was time to go home.

"John, look!" Sally said, pointing out the window beside her.

To their right was an ice-cream parlor. Metal chairs and round tables with thin wire legs were set in front of the store under a yellow awning. At one of the tables sat an elderly couple. The man sat straight in his chair like an army officer, his hair iron-gray and neatly parted, his eyebrows thick. He was keeping time to the music of the band with the cane in his right hand. His left hand held the hand of a little old woman in a black dress, who gazed at him as she sipped from the soda in front of her.

The music was louder here. Just to the north of the town hall, they could see now, was a bandstand with a conical roof. On the bandstand sat half a dozen old men in uniforms, playing instruments. Another man in uniform stood in front of them, waving a baton. It was a moment before John realized what was wrong with the scene. The music was louder and richer than the half-dozen musicians could have produced.

But it was Johnny who pointed out the tape recorder beside the bandstand, "Just like Daddy's."

It turned out that Buffalo Street was not three blocks north of the square but three blocks south.

The aging process had been kind to Mrs. Henry Plummer. She was a small woman, and the retreating years had left their detritus of fat, but the extra weight seemed no burden on her small bones and the cushioning beneath the skin kept it plump and un-wrinkled. Her youthful complexion seemed strangely at odds with her blue-white curls. Her eyes, though, were unmistakably old. They were faded like a blue gingham dress.

They looked at Sally now, John thought, as if to say, "What I have seen you through, my dear, the colic and the boys, the measles and the mumps and the chickenpox and the boys, the frozen fingers and the skinned knees and the boys, the parties and the late hours and the boys. . . . And now you come again to me, bringing this larger, distant boy that I do not like very much, who has taken you from me and treated you with crude familiarity, and you ask me to call him by his first name and consider him one of the family. It's too much."

When she spoke, her voice was surprisingly small. "Henry," she said, a little girl in an old body, "don't stand there talking all day. Take in the bags! These children must be starved to death!"

Henry Plummer had grown thinner as his wife had filled out, as if she had grown fat at his expense. Plummer had been a junior executive long after he had passed in age most of the senior executives, in a firm that manufactured games and toys; but a small inheritance and cautious investments in municipal bonds and life insurance had made possible his com-fortable retirement.

He could not shake the habits of a lifetime; his face bore the wry expression of a man who expects the worst and receives it. He said little, and when he spoke, it was usually to protest. "Well, I guess I'm not the one holding them up," he said, but he stooped for the bags.

John moved quickly to reach the bags first. "I'll get them, Dad," he said. The word "Dad" came out as if it were fitted with rusty hooks. He had never known what to call Henry Plummer. His own father had died when he was a small child, and his mother had died when he was in college; but he could not find in himself any filial affection for Plummer. He disliked the coyness of "Dad," but it was better than the stiffness of "Mr. Plummer" or the false comaraderie of "Henry."

With Mrs. Plummer the problem had not been so great. John recalled a joke from the book he had edited recently for the paperback publishing firm that employed him. "For the first year I said, 'Hey, you!' and then I called her 'Grandma.'"

He straightened with the scuffed suitcases, looking helplessly at Sally for a moment and then apologetically at Plummer. "I guess you've carried your share of luggage already."

"He's perfectly fit," Mrs. Plummer said.

Sally looked only at Johnny. Sally was small and dark-haired and pretty, and John loved her and her whims—"a whim of iron," they called her firm conviction that she knew the right thing to do at any time, in any situation—but when she was around her mother, John saw reflected in her behavior all the traits that he found irritating in the old woman. Sometime, perhaps, she would even be plump like her mother, but now it did not seem likely. She ran after Johnny fourteen hours a day.

She held the hand of her four-year-old, her face flushed, her eyes bright with pride. "I guess you see how he's grown, Mother. Ten pounds since you saw him last Christmas. And three inches taller. Give your grandmother a kiss, Johnny. A big kiss for Grammy. He's been talking all the way from New York about coming to visit Grammy—and Granddad, too, of course. I can't imagine what makes him act so shy now. Usually he isn't. Not even with strangers. Give Grammy a great big kiss."

"Well," Mrs. Plummer said, "you must be starved. Come on in. I've got a ham on the stove, and we'll have sandwiches and coffee. And, Johnny, I've got something for you. A box of chocolates, all your own."

"Oh, Mother!" Sally said. "Not just before lunch. He won't eat a bite."

Johnny jumped up and down. He pulled his hand free from his mother's and ran to Mrs. Plummer. "Candy! Candy!" he shouted. He gave Mrs. Plummer a big wet kiss.

John stood at the living room window listening to the whisper of the air conditioning and looking out at the Florida evening. He could see Johnny playing in the pile of sand his thoughtful grandparents had dumped in the backyard. It had been a relief to be alone with his wife, but now the heavy silence of disagreement hung in the air between them. He had wanted to leave, to return to New York, and she would not even consider the possibility.

He had massed all his arguments, all his uneasiness, about this strange, nightmarish town, about how he felt unwanted, about how it disliked them, and Sally had found his words first amusing and then disagreeable. For her, Sunset Acres was an arcadia for the aged. Her reaction was strongly influenced by that glimpse of the old couple at the ice-cream parlor.

John had always found in her a kind of Walt Disney sentimentality, but it had never disturbed him before. He turned and made one last effort. "Besides, your parents don't even want us here. We've been here only a couple of hours and already they've left us to go to some meeting."

"It's their monthly town hall meeting," Sally said. "They have an obligation to attend. It's part of their self-government or something."

"Oh, hell," John said, turning back to the window. He looked from left to right and back again. "Johnny's gone."

He ran to the back door and fumbled with it for a moment. Then it opened, and he was in the backyard. After the sterile chill of the house, the air outside seemed ripe with warm black earth and green things springing through the soil. The sandpile was empty; there was no place for the boy to hide among the colorful Florida shrubs which hid the backyard of the house behind and had colorful names he could never remember.

John ran around the corner of the house. He reached the porch just as Sally came through the front door.

"There he is," Sally cried out.

"Johnny!" John shouted.

The four-year-old had started across the street. He turned and looked back at them. "Grammy," he said.

John heard him clearly.

The car slipped into the scene like a shadow, silent, unsuspected. John saw it out of the corner of his eye. Later he thought that it must have turned the nearby corner, or perhaps it came out of a driveway. In the moment before the accident, he saw that the old woman in the wide-brimmed hat was driving the car herself. He saw her head turn toward Johnny, and he saw the upright electric turn sharply toward the child.

The front fender hit Johnny and threw him toward the sidewalk. John looked incredulously at the old woman. She smiled at him, and then the car was gone down the street.

"Johnny!" Sally screamed. Already she was in the street, the boy's head cradled in her lap. She hugged him and then pushed him away to look blindly into his face and then hugged him again, rocking him in her arms, crying.

John found himself beside her, kneeling. He pried the boy away from her. Johnny's eyes were closed. His face was pale, but John couldn't find any blood. He lifted the boy's eyelids. The pupils seemed dilated. Johnny did not stir.

"What's the matter with him?" Sally screamed at John. "He's going to die, isn't he?"

"I don't know. Let me think! Let's get him into the house."

"You aren't supposed to move people who've been in an accident!"

"We can't leave him here to be run over by someone else."

John picked up his son gently and walked to the house. He lowered the boy onto the quilt in the front bedroom and looked down at him for a moment. The boy was breathing raggedly. He moaned. His hand twitched. "I've got to get a doctor," John said. "Where's the telephone?"

Sally stared at him as if she hadn't heard. John turned away and looked in the living room. An antique apparatus on a wooden frame was attached to one wall. He picked up the receiver and cranked the handle vigorously. "Hello!" No answer.

He returned to the bedroom. Sally was still standing beside the bed. "What a lousy town!" he said. "No telephone service!" Sally looked at him. She blinked.

"I'll have to go to town," John said. "You stay with Johnny. Keep him warm. Put cold compresses on his head." They might not help Johnny, he thought, but they would keep Sally quiet.

She nodded and headed toward the bathroom.

When he got to the car, it refused to start. After a few attempts, he gave up, knowing he had flooded the motor. He ran back to the house. Sally looked up at him, calmer now that her hands were busy.

"I'm going to run," he told her. "I might see that woman and be unable to resist the impulse to smash into her."

"Don't talk crazy," Sally said. "It was just an accident."

"It was no accident," John said. "I'll be back with a doctor as soon as I can find one."

John ran down the brick sidewalk until his throat burned and then walked for a few steps before breaking once more into a run. By then the square was in sight. The sun had plunged into the Gulf of Mexico, and the town was filled with silence and shadows.

The storefronts were dark. There was no light anywhere in the square.

The first store was a butcher shop. Hams hung in the windows and plucked chickens, naked and scrawny, dangled by cords around their yellow feet. John thought he smelled sawdust and blood. He remembered Johnny and felt sick.

Next was a clothing store with two wide windows under the name "Emporium." In the windows were stiff waxen dummies in black suits and high starched collars; in lace and parasol. Then came a narrow door; on its window were printed the words, "Saunders and Jones, Attorneys at Law." The window framed dark steps.

Beside it was a print shop—piles of paper pads in the window—white, yellow, pink, blue; reams of paper in dusty wrappers; faded invitations and personal cards; and behind them the lurking shapes of printing presses and racks of type.

John passed a narrow bookstore with books stacked high in the window and ranged in ranks into the darkness. Then came a restaurant; a light in the back revealed scattered tables with checkered cloths. He pounded at the door, making a shocking racket in the silence of the square, but no one came.

Kitty-corner across the street, he saw the place and recognized it by the tall, intricately shaped bottles of colored water in the window and the fancy jar hanging from chains. He ran across the brick street and beat on the door with his fist. There was no response. He kicked it, but the drugstore remained silent and dark. Only the echoes answered his summons, and they soon died away.

Next to the drugstore was another dark door. The

words printed across the window in it said, "Joseph M. Bronson, M.D." And underneath, "Geriatrics Only."

John knocked, sure it was useless, wondering, "Why is the town locked up? Where is everybody?" And then he remembered the meeting. That's where everyone was, at the meeting the Plummers couldn't miss. No one could miss the meeting. Everyone had to be there, apparently, even the telephone operator. But where was it being held?

Of course. Where else would a town meeting be held? In the town hall.

He ran across the street once more and up the wide steps. He pulled open one of the heavy doors and stepped into a hall with tall ceilings. Stairways led up on either side, but light came through a pair of doors ahead. He heard a babble of voices. John walked toward the doors, feeling the slick oak floors under his feet, smelling the public toilet odors of old urine and disinfectant.

He stopped for a moment at the doors to peer between them, hoping to see the Plummers, hoping they were close enough to signal without disturbing the others. The old people would be startled if he burst in among them. There would be confusion and explanations, accusations perhaps. He needed a doctor, not an argument.

The room was filled with wooden folding chairs placed neatly in rows, with a wide aisle in the middle and a narrower one on either side. From the backs of the chairs hung shawls and canes. The room had for John the unreal quality of an etching, perhaps because all the backs of the heads that he saw were silver and gray, here and there accented with tints of blue or green.

At the front of the room was a walnut rostrum on a broad platform. Behind the rostrum stood the old man Sally had pointed out in the ice-cream parlor. He stood as straight as he had sat.

The room buzzed as if it had a voice of its own, and the voice rose and fell, faded and returned, the way it does in a dream. One should be able to understand it, one had to understand it, but one couldn't quite make out the words.

The old man banged on the rostrum with a wooden gavel; the gavel had a small silver plate attached to its head. "Everyone will have his chance to be heard," he said. It was like an order. The buzz faded away. "Meanwhile we will speak one at a time, and in a proper manner, first being recognized by the chair.

"Just one moment, Mr. Samuelson.

"For many years the public press has allowed its columns to bleed over the voting age. 'If a boy of eighteen is old enough to die for his country, he is old enough to vote for its legislators,' the sentimentalists have written.

"Nonsense. It takes no intelligence to die. Any idiot can do it. Surviving takes brains. Men of eighteen aren't even old enough to take orders properly, and until a man can take orders, he can't give them.

"Mrs. Richards, I have the floor. When I have finished, I will recognize each of you in turn."

John started to push through the doors and announce the emergency to the entire group, but something about the stillness of the audience paralyzed his decision. He stood there, his hand on the door, his eyes searching for the Plummers.

"Let me finish," the old man at the rostrum said. "Only when a man has attained true maturity—fifty is the earliest date for the start of this time of life—does he begin to identify the important things in life. At this age, the realization comes to him, if it ever comes, that the individual has the right to protect and preserve the property that he has accumulated by his own hard work, and, in the protection of this right, the state stands between the individual and mob rule in Washington. Upon these eternal values we take our stand: the individual, his property, and state's rights. Else our civilization, and everything in it of value, will perish."

The light faded from his eyes, and the gavel which had been raised in his hand like a saber sank to the rostrum. "Mr. Samuelson."

In the front of the room a man stood up. He was small and bald except for two small tufts of hair above his ears. "I have heard what you said, and I understand what you said because you said it before. It is all very well to talk of the rights of the individual to protect his property, but how can he protect his property when the government taxes and taxes and taxes—state governments as well as Washington? I say, 'Let the government give us four exemptions instead of two.'"

A cracked voice in the back of the room said, "Let them cut out taxes altogether for senior citizens!"

"Yes!"

"No!"

A small, thin woman got up in the middle of the audience. "Four hundred dollars a month for every man and woman over sixty-five!" she said flatly. "Why shouldn't we have it? Didn't we build this country?

Let the government give us back a little of what they have taken away. Besides, think of the money it would put into circulation."

"You have not been recognized, Mrs. Richards," the chairman said, "and I declare you out of order and the Townsendites as well. What you are advocating is socialism, more government, not less."

"Reds!" someone shouted. "Commies!" said someone else. "That's not true!" said a woman near the door. "It's only fair," shouted an old man, nodding vigorously. Canes and crutches were waved in the air, a hundred Excaliburs and no Arthur. John glanced behind him to see if the way was clear for retreat in case real violence broke out.

"Sally!" he exclaimed, discovering her behind him. "What are you doing here? Where's Johnny?"

"He's in the car. He woke up. He seemed all right. I thought I'd better find you. Then we'd be closer to the doctor. I looked all over. What are you doing here?"

John rubbed his forehead. "I don't know. I was looking for a doctor. Something's going on here. I don't know what it is, but I don't like it."

"What's going on?"

Sally tried to push past him, but John grabbed her arm. "Don't go in there!"

The chairman's gavel finally brought order out of confusion. "We are senior citizens, not young hoodlums!" he admonished them. "We can disagree without forgetting our dignity and our common interests. Mrs. Johnson."

A woman stood up at the right beside one of the tall windows that now framed the night. She was a stout woman with gray hair pulled back into a bun. "It seems to me, Colonel, that we are getting far from the subject of this meeting—indeed, the subject of all our meetings—and that is what we are going to do about the young people who are taking over everything and pushing us out. As many of you know, I have no prejudices about young people. Some of my best friends are young people, and, although I cannot name my children among them, for they are ingrates, I bear my son and my two daughters no ill will."

She paused for a deep breath. "We must not let the young people get the upper hand. We must find ways of ensuring that we get from them the proper respect for our age and our experience. The best way to do this, I believe, is to keep them in suspense about the property—the one thing about us they still value—how much there is and what will become of it. Myself, I pretend that there is at least two or three times as much. When I am visiting one of them, I leave my checkbook lying carelessly about—the one that has the very large and false balance. And I let them overhear me make an appointment to see a lawyer. What do I have to see a lawyer about, they think, except my will?

"Actually I have written my will once and for all, leaving my property to the Good Samaritan Rest Home for the Aged, and I do not intend to change it. But I worry that some clever young lawyer will find a way to break the will. They're always doing that when you disinherit someone."

"Mrs. Johnson," the Colonel said, "you have a whole town full of friends who will testify that you always have been in full possession of your faculties, if it ever should come to that, God forbid! Mrs. Fredericks?"

"Nasty old woman," Sally muttered. "Where are Mother and Father? I don't see them. I don't think they're here at all."

"Sh-h-h!"

"I'm leaving my money to my cat," said a bent old woman with a hearing aid in her ear. "I'm just sorry I won't get to see their faces."

The Colonel smiled at her as he nodded her back to her seat at the left front. Then he recognized a man sitting in the front row. "Mr. Saunders."

The man who arose was short, straight, and precise. "I would like to remind these ladies of the services of our legal aid department. We have had good luck in constructing unbreakable legal documents. A word of caution, however—the more far-fetched the legatee, though to be sure the more satisfying, the more likely the breaking of the will. There is only one certain way to prevent property from falling into the hands of those who have neither worked for it nor merited it—and that is to spend it.

"Personally, I am determined to spend on the good life every cent that I accumulated in a long and —you will pardon my lack of humility—distinguished career at the bar."

"Your personal life is your own concern, Mr. Saunders," the Colonel said, "but I must tell you, sir, that we are aware of how you spend your money and your time away from here. I do not recommend it to others, nor do I approve of your presenting it to us as worthy of emulation. Indeed, I think you do our cause damage."

Mr. Saunders had not resumed his seat. He bowed

and continued, "Each to his own tastes—I cite an effective method for keeping the younger generation in check. There are other ways of disposing of property irretrievably." He sat down.

John pulled Sally back from the doors. "Go to the car," he said. "Get out of here. Go back to the house and get our bags packed. Quick!"

"Mrs. Plummer?" the Colonel said.

Sally pulled away from John.

The familiar figure stood up at the front of the room. Now John could identify beside her the gray head of Henry Plummer, turned now toward the plump face of his wife.

"We all remember," Mrs. Plummer said calmly, "what a trial children are. What we may forget is that our children have children. I do my best not to let my daughter forget the torments she inflicted upon me when she was a child. We hide these things from them. We conceal the bitterness. They seldom suspect. And we take our revenge, if we are wise, by encouraging their children to be just as great a trial to their parents. We give them candy before meals. We encourage them to talk back to their parents. We build up their infant egos so that they will stand up for their childish rights. When their parents try to punish them, we stand between the child and the punishment. Fellow senior citizens, this is our revenge: that their parents will be as miserable as we were."

"Mother! No!" Sally cried out.

The words and the youthful voice that spoke them rippled the audience like a stone tossed into a pond. Faces turned toward the back of the meeting room, faces with wrinkles and white hair and faded eyes, faces searching, nearsighted, faces disturbed, faces beginning to fear and to hate. Among them was one face John knew well, a face that had dissembled malice and masqueraded malevolence as devotion.

"Do as I told you!" John said violently. "Get out of here!"

For once in her life, Sally did as she was told. She ran down the hall, pushed her way through the big front doors, and was gone. John looked for something with which to bar the doors to the meeting room, but the hall was bare. He was turning back to the doors when he saw the oak cane in the corner. He caught it up and slipped it through the handles. Then he put his shoulder against the doors.

In the meeting room the gathering emotion was beginning to whip thin blood into a simulation of youthful vigor, and treble voices began to deepen as they shouted encouragement at those nearest the doors. "A spy!"

"Was it a woman?"

"A girl."

"Let me get my hands on her!"

The first wave hit the doors. John was knocked off balance. He pushed himself forward again, and again the surge of bodies against the other side forced him back. He dug in his feet and shoved. A sound of commotion added to the shouting in the meeting room. John heard something—or someone—fall.

The next time he was forced from the doors, the cane bent. Again he pushed the doors shut; the cane straightened. At the same moment he felt a sharp pain across his back. He looked back. The Colonel was behind him, breathing hard, the glow of combat in his eyes and the cane in his hand upraised for another blow, like the hand of Abraham over Isaac.

John stepped back. In his hand he found the cane that had been thrust through the door handles. He raised it over his head as the Colonel struck again. The blow fell upon the cane. The Colonel drew back his cane and swung once more, and again his blow was parried, more by accident than skill. Then the doors burst open, and the wild old bodies were upon them.

John caught brief glimpses of flying white hair and ripped lace and spectacles worn awry. Canes and crutches were raised above him. He smelled lavender and bay rum mixed with the sweet-sour odor of sweat. He heard shrill voices, like the voices of children, cry out curses and maledictions, and he felt upon various parts of his body the blows of feeble fists, their bones scarcely padded, doing perhaps more damage to themselves than to him, though it seemed sufficient.

He went down quickly. Rather too quickly, he thought dazedly as he lay upon the floor, curled into a fetal position to avoid the stamping feet and kicks and makeshift clubs.

He kept waiting for it to be over, for consciousness to leave him, but most of the blows missed him, and in the confusion and the milling about, the object of the hatred was lost. John saw a corridor that led between bodies and legs through the doors that opened into the meeting room. He crawled by inches toward the room; eventually he found himself among the chairs. The commotion was behind him.

Cautiously he peered over the top of a fallen chair. He saw what he had overlooked before—a door behind the rostrum. It stood open to the night. That was how the Colonel, with instinctive strategy, had come up behind him, he thought, and he crept toward it and down the narrow steps behind the town hall.

For a moment he stood in the darkness assessing his injuries. He was surprised: they were few, none serious. Perhaps tomorrow he would find bruises enough and a lump here and there and perhaps even a broken rib or two, but now there was only a little pain. He started to run.

He had been running in the darkness for a long time, not certain he was running in the right direction, not sure he knew what the right direction was, when a dark shape coasted up beside him. He dodged instinctively before he recognized the sound of the motor.

"John!" It was a voice he knew. "John?"

The Volkswagen was running without lights. John caught the door handle. The door came open. The car stopped. "Move over," he said, out of breath. Sally climbed over the gear shift, and John slid into the bucket seat. He released the hand brake and pushed hard on the accelerator. The car plunged forward.

Only when they reached the highway did John speak again. "Is Johnny all right?"

"I think so," Sally said. "But he's got to see a doctor."

"We'll find a doctor in Orange Grove."

"A young one."

John wiped his nose on the back of his hand and looked at it. His hand was smeared with blood. "Damn!"

She pressed a tissue into his hand. "Was it bad?"

"Incredible!" He laughed harshly and said it again

in a different tone. "Incredible. What a day! And what a night! But it's over. And a lot of other things are over."

Johnny was crying in the back seat.

"What do you mean?" Sally asked. "Hush, Johnny, it's going to be all right."

"Grammy!" Johnny moaned.

"The letters. Presents for people who don't need anything. Worrying about what mother's going to think. . . ."

The car slowed as John looked back toward the peaceful town of Sunset Acres, sleeping now in the Florida night, and remembered the wide lawns and the broad porches, the brick streets and the slow time, and the old folks. "All over," he said again.

Johnny was still crying.

"Shut up, Johnny!" he said between his teeth and immediately felt guilty.

"John!" Sally said. "We mustn't ever be like that toward our son."

She wasn't referring just to what he had said, John knew. He glanced back toward the small figure huddled in the back seat. It wasn't over, he thought; it was beginning. "It's over," he said again, as if he could convince himself by repetition. Sally was silent. "Why don't you say something?" John asked.

"I keep thinking about how it used to be," she said. "He's my father. She's my mother. How can anything change that? You can't expect me to hate my own father and mother?"

It wasn't over. It would never be over. Even though the children sometimes escaped, the old folks always won: the children grew up; the young people became old folks.

The car speeded up and rushed through the night, the headlights carving a corridor through the darkness, a corridor that kept closing behind them. The corridor still was there, as real in back as it was revealing in front, and it could never be closed.